J
♥
J
♣
J
♦
J
♠
QUEEN OF JACKS
Kyleef Watts

Queen of Jacks

By: Kyleef Watts

Cover Created by Jazzy Kitty Publishing

Cover Designed by Kyleef Watts

Logo Designs by Andre M. Saunders/Jess Zimmerman

Editor: Anelda L. Attaway

© 2016 Kyleef Watts

ISBN 978-0-9970848-9-4

Library of Congress Control Number: 2016949877

ACKNOWLEDGMENTS

First and foremost, I'd like to give thanks to the Creator for all that was, is and will be, for my gifts, blessings, trials, and tribulations!

To my Grandmom Clara Lee Warren. Thank you for intervening on my behalf up there, I love you!

To my Rock my Mother Alethia Watts. Without you showing me the true meaning of love, patience, humbleness, strength, sacrifice, and faith, I KNOW I wouldn't be alive or in my right state of mind. Thank You Mommy, I love you!

Thanks to a beautiful and intelligent young lady that NEVER gave up on me, even at my lowest. My first born Kadeisha Custis.

Angie Warren, I love you, thanks for having my back since I've been on this earth.

To my Brother Kentae Watts, I GOT YOU! Words aren't needed.

Marshona Morris, I'm older but you inspire me to rise.

Iya Jones, Sis I love you. You keep me sharp!

A great thanks to Yusef Matthews, Lil Sporty (Harlee Watts), K Dog (Kashawn Weston), Coco (Cory Bailey), My crew Triple A, O.G. J Rock, Herc, Ricky D, and Demond.

Last but not least, my publisher Anelda Attaway and her staff at Jazzy Kitty Publishing.

DEDICATIONS

This book is dedicated to my beautiful daughters Kadeisha, Kyleyah, Kalayah, Keimora, Kyra and Baby K. You all make me a rich man without having money.

TABLE OF CONTENTS

TABLE OF CONTENTS

TABLE OF CONTENTS

As Lana awoke she felt her body thrashing, and a yell escaped her mouth. She sat up looking around startled and dazed. Lana went to move her hair out of her face and felt a heavy bandage on her right hand. She looked at her hand as if it were a King Cobra. Suddenly, she heard something stir to her left and her head snapped in that direction. The noise came from a man sleep in a recliner with his face hidden beneath some covers. Lana thought hard and looked over the room again. She was in a hospital and that was her cousin "X" asleep in the chair in the corner. It all hit her like a 44 slug in the chest. As she put her left hand over her mouth, suppressing a scream as her dormant memories surfaced. Tears came down her face as she recalled the painful event that put her in this hospital bed and everything that lead up to it.

2 YEARS EARLIER

Kalana Watson was 5'4" with soft cocoa butter complexion and long shoulder length jet black hair that turned violet every summer. Her eyes had a hazel color, the same color as her mother's. She was definitely a "dime" even though she never wore skin tight clothing. Lana had an athletic hourglass shaped body that she concealed properly. She had just graduated from Seaford High the week before. Lana went to Ocean City like all the graduates do every year. Letting off some steam, most of the kid's partied hard. Lana only attended two parties during the whole week. She mostly just sat on the beach and reflected, thinking of her future. Today is Lana's first day back to work at Boscov's in the Salisbury Mall. Work definitely wasn't on her mind; she was thinking about her tuition fee. Lana had been accepted to Delaware State University, and she was determined to attend, but between her and her mother they only had the money for the first two semesters covered. Lana was worried. She already planned on commuting which would save money but it still wasn't adding up. Lana already wished she could relieve her overworked single parenting mother. Lana's father had killed himself in the late 90s after he had been laid off from DuPont. Up until her father's death, life was perfect for Lanie, as her father use to call her. DuPont paid at that time $25 an hour, but by the late 90s the company was closing its doors on their Seaford DE Plant. With bills backing up and a family to provide for Lana's father saw no way out but suicide. A customer's loud sigh snapped Lana out of her financial woes funk.

"Excuse me, I'm sorry," Lana asked, "may I help you?"

"Yes, you certainly may," said a snobbish middle-aged White woman.

Lana said to herself that she was sick of these arrogant women, but she had to give this one her props. The lady looked like new money with her Mary Katrantzou fit and flare dress, Stella McCartney clutch, and bow-front Christian Louboutin pumps. Lana knew her fashion.

"I'd like to purchase two pairs of these platform sandals."

"That'll be $179.00," Lana said.

"Thank you, and keep the change," the lady said as she ran off in a hurry.

Lana was grateful for the tip but wanted so bad to be giving tips instead of receiving them. Lana's co-worker Kisha came over.

"Lana, I'm so proud of you," Kisha said, "I've got a surprise for you!"

"What is it girl, tell me!" Lana asked excitedly.

"Okay," Kisha continued, "VIP tickets to the Rick Ross concert!" Lana let out a tiny squeal as she embraced Kisha.

"Thank you, you know I love Rick Ross and I've never been to a concert."

"I know girl, the only catch is, you gotta take me."

Kisha was 29, she was also Lana's trainer when she started working at Boscov's. Lana loved her. Kisha always kept it real and told Lana the truth no matter how hard it was to swallow.

"Okay, you know we gonna be the fliest in the building," said Kisha and hugged Lana tight again then held her at arm's length.

"I know you're worried about paying for school, but don't, it's going to be alright. The Lord finds a way for good people baby."

Lana couldn't help but sometimes think her dreams were far-fetched. She wanted a successful and prosperous career and life; not a life with a dead-end job with no future. Lana smiled but looked away from Kish's hopeful eyes, wishing that her friend was right.

"I know everything's gonna be alright Kish, cause I'm gonna work my butt off," Lana said with a smile finally spreading across her lips.

Kish clapped her hands with delight.

"That's my girl, I know you gonna do your thang!"

As both ladies went back to their respective jobs, Lana felt ecstatic. Talks with Kisha always made Lana feel good and like she could conquer the world. She wiped the smudges and fingerprints off the display counters while humming a tune by Jill Scott. Lana spent the remainder of her work daydreaming of her future. She dreamt of being so successful that she told her mom to retire from her job. She also saw herself coming home to a huge mansion with foreign cars and designer clothes. Lana envisioned all the gains that came with having money. The only problem she hadn't envisioned was what she would be doing to make all of this money.

CHAPTER 1

"What you find?"

"There's no alarm sign or wires on the windows."

"Any dogs?"

"Naw didn't see any doghouse or hear any in the house."

"Alright, is anyone up?"

"I see a TV. on in just one of the bedrooms, it's the master bedroom too."

"Okay, let's move, you know what to do and how to do it!"

Everything was said in low whispers between X and his young boy D. They were doing what they do best, about to run up in a "dope boys" house. What would be insane to most people was routine to these two and normal. X quarterbacked all the capers, his youngin' D just had to have the heart to roll with and trust him. Indeed, D trusted X…with his life. They've been robbing hustlers together for about three years. They'd actually lost count on how many jux they'd done.

X always said, "A good caper must have an inside man." Which brings us to their present heist.

THE HEIST

The inside man, or rather a woman, for this particular job, said dude keeps two safes in the house that she knows of, one in the bedroom closet and the other one in the garage. The safe in the bedroom has the cash and the one in the garage has the coke. X at 6 feet 3 inches and 260 lbs., always took care of the door. One massive kick from X's size 14 boot to the center of the door made it cave in like it was made of paper. BOOM! "Police!" X and D yelled to freeze their victim. D's in first, followed by X.

From their inside girl they already knew the layout of the house and how many people were there. Crouched down low X & D moved with speed, with their pistols held out. They both made their way to the master bedroom. Just as X and D swung their pistols into the bedroom, they spotted a fat dark skinned man and a thick Ass light-skinned woman with blond hair buck naked. The fat man was reaching towards a nightstand next to the bed. Before the fat man could open the drawer, X had smacked the man with his 357.

As the fat man laid back on the bed holding his face, blood leaked through his hands, down his chest. The blond stared wide-eyed and screamed. D was on her in a flash. He ducked taped her mouth then took her to the bathroom and tied her up in the tub. X held the fat man at gunpoint waiting for D to return. As soon as D returned, he hogged tied the fat man and taped his mouth. The man was a big like the man on Jake and the Fatman so D had a time, but finally the fat man was secured. Everything seemed to have to happen in less than 20 seconds without a word being spoken from X and D.

With the fat man lying on the floor, X finally spoke, "We need the bread and the dope!" The fat man was drenched in blood and sweat. He looked like he could kill with his eyes. He watched closely as the smaller masked man passed the bigger one an object.

"If you say anything other than where the dope or bread is, I'm taking this!"

X held up what was handed to him from D, it was an ice pick. X roughly tore the fat man's boxers off.

"And stick it as far as I can in your pee pee! Shake your head if you understand!" The fat man's whole body shook as he rigorously nodded.

"For starters, where's the money?" X asked as he moved the tape off the fat man's mouth.

"It's in the closet, in the floor, under my wife's shoes, please don…" X put the tape back over his mouth and motioned towards D. D moved toward the closet after knocking down clothes and throwing shoes. He came out with a safe about the size of a small suitcase.

"Okay, where's the dope?" X removed the tape once more. This time, the fat man hesitated with his answer. Before he could spit a lie out of his lips, X grabbed his Johnson and was pushing the ice pick ever so close to his pee hole.

"ALRIGHT! ALRIGHT! It's in the garage!"

X wasn't short for Xavier, it stood for "Executioner!" Born Yusef Watson, he migrated all over Sussex County in his early teens, but his homes were the Notorious C-Roc and Flamboyant Block 3rd and North before its demise. There wasn't a past memory in X's head where he couldn't remember as a child a time his mother wasn't getting high. His mother overdosed in 1996. With X already providing for himself, her death just made him dive deeper into the underworld, and the little conscience he had for another human evaporated. X had seen hustlers all his life, either the grimy go-getters from the "ROC" or the finesse and flashiness of 3rd North's crew. So hustling was all he knew and grew to love. X and his right-hand man Kush started selling crack at age 13. All these years later they're still considered brothers and are tighter than ever. In their "Family" everyone plays their part!

"Man I thought you were gonna castrate that nigga, ha-ha," D said laughing. He was driving them to a safe house so they could break down the money and coke.

"Dog, you know I wasn't gonna fuck homeboy up like that, had to fake the funk tho, ha, ha, ha, ha!" They rode with no music in the squatter, focused on making it safe to their destination.

D pulled into a long dirt lane on a back road in Dodge City. After they rode down the lane for a minute, a small house appeared. D pulled around the back of it and cut the engine off. He sat in silence because he knew X would be saying prayers.

After a couple minutes, X tucked his beads and said, "Alright Dog, don't be in here talking bout' what we just did."

"Why not, she knows what we do anyway!"

"That ain't the point, as long as people don't see it or hear it from our lips, we never did it…okay? Get the bags Nigga, and don't open nothing until we at the table. I don't trust your Ass!" X said as he laughed. As X opened the back door to the house, "good green" hit 'em in the face. He inhaled and smiled.

"That better be my "young bull" creeping up in here," said in a high-pitched sweet voice. Ella B came into the kitchen as X and D were removing their boots and overalls. Ella B was one of those moms from the old school.

She asked, "What up D?" as she hugged X, "I was about to go to sleep on y'all." She talked as they headed to the dining room's "big round table."

"I already rolled some blueberry for you, there go the board and you know where the Pyrex is."

X spoke smiling, "That's why you my Baby Ms. B, you already know what a nigga need." He kissed her on the cheek as she smiled.

"I'm going to bed, it's 3 in the morning, and y'all Niggas gon' be up all night. Leave me what's mine on the table. Goodnight." D and X were grinning like little boys up to no good as they both grabbed a duffle bag and emptied it weighing and separating everything.

"33 ounces of "Girl," and 22 stacks," X said as he leaned back blowing smoke out of his nose.

First X gave Lil D his cut of the money and coke. Then he put the inside girl's money to the side. That's all she wanted was money, which was cool. The rest of the money was his, he put a stack on the table for Ella B and an ounce. Then he took a couple ounces for himself. The rest will go to his best friend Kush. EVERYONE PLAYS THEIR PART!

THE CELEBRATION

"Hood Billionaire, Hood Billionaire, Hood Billionaire!" X's ringtone took him from his thoughts of what lies ahead for his day.

"What up Lost, its 7 in the morning what you up to?" X asked grinning at hearing the voice of one of his young boys.

"You know money don't sleep Nigga, anyway, you know Piff Boys bringing Ross up tonight. I know you coming!"

"Hell yeah, you know I Fucks with Rozay! I got these things for you too, whenever you ready."

"Okay," the dreadlocked youngin' Lost said; who got his name because he resembled members of the group the Lost Boyz.

"I be needing that!" Lost continued, "but Nigga, be at the Civic Center by 10. I'll meet you at the door."

"Okay," X said, "be easy Bro."

"Remember, don't miss Rick Ross at our own Salisbury Civic Center, TONIGHT! Opening for Ricky Rozay TONIGHT will be Gold Trigga and the Piff Boys! Bought to you by Piff Boys Ent. Rick Ross TONIGHT!!" The radio DJ screamed through the speakers before playing an old school Mary J. Blige song. Lana and Kish sang along while Lana finished up Kish's hair and sipped Moscato. They were over Kish's house getting ready for the big concert.

Kish demanded to Lana earlier that day, "Tonight we ain't having no worries, Girl. So, forget about school, work, bills and the rest of the Bullshit, we partying tonight!" That speech had solidified Lana's plans; she had already let Kish talk her into hitting the blunt a couple times.

She thought to herself, "I'm just going to have fun tonight."

"Girl you hooked a Bitch up tonight!" Kish said as she looked in a mirror.

"You know I'm the Shit," Lana said while smacking Kish's extended hand.

"Oh Shit Girl, what time is it?" Kish asked, "we have to get dressed and get up out of here!"

"Come on Nigga, I want to see Trig perform!" X hollered. D did a double take as he was sliding into X's black on black Caddy.

"Nigga you sharp ain't you?"

"Just a little something youngin'… Fuck with me and I'll school you! Now roll that Shit up!" X said laughing, "and I got…BOOM!" X flashed a couple white capsules at D.

"Aw Shit, you got the mollies on deck!" They both popped one and sipped some Belair that X had and rode out bumping "Bad Man" by Freak Dollaz.

Lana had never seen this many people in her life at one place before. Their VIP tickets got them through the doors fast and escorted to their seats in the third row. Lana and Kish fronted like they didn't see all the heads turning as they "cat walked" to their seats. They just knew they were "fresh to death" from head to heels. Lana wore her silky jet-black hair down to her shoulders. Rocking a beige Chanel dress that slanted from one thick thigh to her knee, with matching open toe heels. Kish loved to show off her curves, she had Ass for days. She wore a black Cavalli catsuit that looked painted on with black stilettos. As they both sat, a bottle of Moet and two glasses were brought to their table.

"This is courtesy of S.C.A. Promotions," a short brown-skinned brother with dreads said to the ladies. He wore all white except for the thin red beads around his neck.

"Thank you so much," Kish said, "you all sure do know how to treat a lady."

"Thanks," he replied, "they call me Lost Boy." Then the man asked, "What's your name?"

She smiled, "Lost-boy?" That's your name? I'm Kish, maybe I can FIND you and turn you into a man." She smiled giving him a seductive look.

"You definitely won't have to look for me Ma, I'll find you later! See you in a few Kisha." Lana bust out laughing when "Lost Boy" left.

"Girl you crazy!"

"What! He was a cute little thang."

"You scared him off all aggressive!"

"Shit…he'll be back…watch!"

"Dog, I'm grooving like a Mutherfucker."

"Me too, I think it was too much molly in them caps," D said.

"Did you text 'Lost' and tell 'em we here?"

"Yeah, he'll be at the door."

X and D avoided the long line that wrapped around the building seem like it was a party outside. *"Bad Bitches everywhere," X thought as his head was on a swivel while he walked towards the doors.* Feeling the effects of the mollies had X and D feeling like "Mack's." X rocked some black Prada shades, black button-down Sean John and black slacks with black Clark's on his feet. D wore POLO as always from head to toe, red, and white. Lost met them at the door. Niggas were everywhere as Lost lead them through the building. All along giving daps and hugs or just acknowledgments to people they knew. X heard his homie Trigga on stage ripping Shit up. They were lead backstage where a lot of X's homies were. Kush and OG were talking to two Spanish girls.

"What's up X?"

"What up Bro." OG passed X a blunt.

X was just passing it back when Lost called him. "Come here X."

"What's up Dog?" He led X to the rear of the stage, just in back of the curtain and DJ booth.

"You know that broad right there Dog?" Lost asked pointing at Kish.

"Naw, but she fine."

"She was on me, but I want the girl she with." Just then X looked to Kisha's right and noticed a familiar face. He took off walking right onto the stage. Lost called after him and then just said Fuck it and followed. They walked around DJ X Lethal; all the time X was squinting to get a better look. In the middle of his rhyme, Gold Trigga gave X and Lost a shot out and some dap. Security approached as X reached the exit of the stage, still staring out into the crowd. Lost assured them everything was good.

"What's up Big Homie?"

"Man get those two and bring 'em backstage!"

"What you gonna put me down with the one I want?"

"Yeah, I got you," X said as he smiled and turned around to go backstage.

Lana and Kisha were listening to the fat boy on stage with the gold gun hanging from his chain. Lana tapped Kisha and pointed her hand in the direction of Lost Boy coming towards them.

"Told you!" Kisha said.

"Are you ladies enjoying yourselves?" They both smiled and said they were.

Lost said, "I would like to give y'all even better seats and a chance to meet Rick Ross personally backstage. Y'all coming?"

Kisha and Lana looked at each other, "sure why not!" They said together.

Lost lead them backstage into a cloud of weed smoke. They saw what look to be a large dice game. Lana pointed out Rick Ross and the light-skinned boy with the dreads that be with him to Kisha, they both were in the game. Lost Boy had told them to have a seat in some chairs about 20 feet from the dice game. Lana and Kisha watched as Lost went over to the game and spoke to a big bald head light-skinned nigga. He shook his head and followed Lost. As X and Lost got closer to Lana and Kisha, X was all teeth, smiling. Lana couldn't believe her eyes and didn't comprehend who he was until he was standing right in front of her. They embraced and held onto each other for a minute. Kisha and Lost looked baffled.

CHAPTER 2

Lana couldn't believe how fast summer flew past. She was so eager and excited when college started for her. But from the get-go, she was financially strained, barely having enough money for her required books. The commute from home to Dover was grueling, plus her job at the mall had cut her hours. More than a few times she had thought about calling her cousin Yusef for a loan but felt they didn't know each other well enough for her to be asking for money. On the other hand, he did say to call him if she needed ANYTHING. She was in her last class of the day, African American History. Even though it was Lana's favorite subject, her mind drifted back to the summer at the concert. Her cuz had introduced her to Rick Ross and afterward she had followed Yusef and his crew to Ocean City.

"We had a ball that night," she thought.

Yusef wouldn't let her or Kish pay for anything. It seemed like him and his boys didn't have a worry in the world, especially about money. "Ms. Watson!! Could you repeat what I just said?" Lana snapped out of her daydream to see that the whole class and Mr. Duker were waiting for her to speak.

"I'm sorry Sir, I wasn't paying attention."

"At least you're honest, but I'll need a three-page report on why paying attention in class is important."

On the ride home Lana debated and struggled with herself on calling Yusef for a loan. The concert had been 5 months ago and before that she hadn't seen him since they were kids up until her father died. On the other hand, they were family and he had made her promise, "If you need anything, call me!"

"Yo, hello, may I speak to Yusef?" Now it was his turn to be speechless because no one called him that.

"Who wants him? I...I'm his cousin, Kalana and..."

"Oh Shit, what up cuz, this MC. How you doing, I've been thinking about you." Little did Lana know X had been thinking about her. Not really about how her well-being was but for his own reasons.

"Yusef, I know we..."

"Lana just call me X cuz..."

"Okay...X, I know we haven't been in touch, but with my school and my job cutting back my hours I...I'm having money problems bad!"

"Say no more cuz, I got you."

"Umm, where you gonna be tomorrow about 12:30?"

"I'll be in Dover. My last class is at 11:00."

I'll see you when I get up there Lanie. Don't worry about no bread cuz, we gon' make it happen Okay?"

"Okay, see you tomorrow."

X had texted Lana earlier and told her to meet him across the street from Del-State at the food court in the Dover Mall. When she arrived at 10 o'clock she spotted X sitting across the small table from a petite light-skinned girl with a short haircut like Halle Berry.

As she approached, X stood up with a big smile, "How you doing cuz?" Opening his arms for a hug.

"Lana, this is Isis and Isis this is my cuz, Lana." Both women greeted one another with a smile and a quick look cover.

Lana said to herself, *"These two looking like a million bucks while I'm looking like a bum in sweats."*

X in his traditional black. He was in an all-black Coogie outfit with red lettering and some butter Timbs. Even from Isis' seated position Lana noticed white Monique Lhuiller cocktail dress.

He said, "Okay then, let's shop and talk."

Isis didn't say much as the three of them walked through the mall. Lana and X caught up on a lot of lost time, answering and asking each other questions about family memories.

Isis finally spoke, "Let's go in Lady's Foot Locker." As X and Lana followed her into the store, X stopped Lana by gently grooming her hand.

"Lana, we family so I'm not gonna sit here and Bullshit with you. I came because you asked for my help and that's cool but also…cause I need your help cuz."

He pointed his head toward Isis, "I want you two to work together. I'll explain more before the days out just keep an open mind, please.

"Lana didn't know what to say or think. She could only imagine what illegal activities X was into. Lana wasn't going to have any part in it.

Before she could speak, Isis yelled, "Lana, what size do you wear?"

"Why?" she said.

"Do you like these?" Isis held up a pink, gray, and black pair of Air Max's.

Lana said, "Yeah but I'm…I'm broke." Isis just waved a hand at her.

"Let me get two pairs of these," she said to the lady in the referee shirt "size 7 and 6."

While Lana just stared in the direction of Isis looking suspicious, X leaned over to her, "We family cuz, that's how our whole team roll."

Before they walked out of the mall Lana and Isis had two dresses a piece by the Kardashian Collection and Gladiator heels by Monika Chiang. Lana was adding in her mind that X must have spent close to 2 grand. She loved to shop and loved the attention but she wasn't a fool and wondered all this at what cost! X still hadn't said what he needed her help with and Lana thought it surely wasn't spending money. All of a sudden, she had bad vibes; a long-lost cousin pops up and is throwing money at her. Lana's mind was racing as Isis and X drove her to her car that was still on campus across from the mall. The suspense was killing her, she couldn't hold back her questions any longer.

"Alright! Alright!! What are you…I mean…where's this money coming from?" she asked as she held up one of the shopping bags from the mall. Isis and X looked at each other and bust out laughing.

"What's funny, why are you laughing at me?" Lana was dead serious as she looked between the both of them.

"That's my car right there." She pointed as Isis drove past the campus security guard shack and took a right into a parking lot.

As they parked beside a 91 Hyundai, X and Isis turned to Lana in the back cocking her head like what? X reached over the seat and tossed a knot of money into her lap. Lana's eyes look liked 50 cent pieces as she looked down at the roll of $100-dollar bills.

"Tell her Ice," X said how looking into Lana's eyes not cracking a smile.

Isis with a devious smile said, "Lana we don't do much, we stick-up doe boys."

VIP

"What up Sexy, what's your name?"

"I'm Lisa, and this is my sister Kim," the blond haired girl said.

The big man that said his name was AG yelled over the music, "Y'all too fine to be down here, y'all should come up to V.I.P. with me and my man."

The two girls followed the big man up some stairs then turned right. As they continued to walk they could see the people on the dance floor down below. AG led them into a room to the left with a circular black leather couch taking up all four sides of the room except the door. There was one man sitting behind a large table that was in the center. He was a slim brown skin guy with cornrows that draped to his shoulders, talking into a cell phone. AG introduced Lisa and Kim to his man Cash but Cash did nothing more than nod and took a swig from his champagne bottle.

AG pressed a button and a couple minutes later a white man in a suit came into the room and asked, "What can I help you with tonight?"

"Bring us two more bottles of Rose he mixed the liquor and the juice."

"Where y'all from? I can look at y'all and tell it ain't Da Bury," Lisa the blond, petite cutie said that they were from "Groove City" and were coming from UMES.

Lisa could feel AG's eyes all over her as he licked his lips. She wanted him to get an eye full, she knew the outfits she chose for her and her girl would do the trick. Black Fendi catsuit for her girl, since she had more curves and a Harvey Leger red bandage dress for her showing her sexy legs and full breast. Cash finally got off his phone, though it continued to ring Craig Mack's old song *"Gotta Get Da Cash, Gotta Get the Doe."*

Cash instantly leaned over to Kim's ear nonchalantly asking, "You gonna let me hit this big Ass tonight or what?" She was just about to cuss him out but remembered she was Kim tonight.

She replied, "Maybe, but I don't think you can handle all this." As she ran her hand from her breast to her thighs and stopping on her soft butt.

Cash's mouth watered as he said, "This is the only night me and my sister are out here, we go back to Groove in the morning, are you gonna show me a good time tonight?"

Cash said, "Hell yeah!" as he picked his phone up that continuously sung that song and turned it off. "Yo, AG we off for the night Dog."

An hour later Lisa was tipsy and feeling good. She was giving AG a seductive slow lap dance while giggling. Cash didn't get a lap dance but he scored a few kisses and his hands were all over Kim.

In the midst of the clouds of purple haze, Kim spoke, "Cash I think we should do this some other time."

"What? I thought we were chilling together all night!"

"My sister looks like she's too drunk to drive and…I'm kinda tired. We'll just catch a cab to our room."

Cash cut her off, "I'll take y'all to the room, we'll just bring y'all back in the morning to pick ya ride up."

Kim creased her brow like she was thinking hard on the decision.

"Okay, but let's get going, I want to feel you inside me."

Cash didn't mind for once not having to pay for a room, even though he was one of the biggest heroin dealers in Salisbury right now.

Cash was the brains and his boy AG, short for Andre da Giant, was the muscle. Once every couple weeks, they would come to the Brew River.

The bouncer from "Da Bricks" informed X that Cash and AG came to the club often. Anthony, the bouncer a.k.a. Big Sexy, called X as soon as their marks walked through the club doors.

As they piled in Cash's Audi R57 he asked, "What hotel y'all in?"

"We at the Days Inn," Kim replied over D-Block blasting out the speakers, while she and Lisa rode in the back seat. When they reached the hotel, the girls said they had left a stick in the back door keeping it open so they didn't have to go past the receptionist. Immediately Cash's spider senses went off.

When the girls jumped out of the car heading to the back door, Cash called AG, "Yo Dog!"

"What up Man, come on?"

"You got your gat?"

"Yeah, but I left it in the car, why?"

"Man we with two fine Ass broads, don't start that paranoid Shit," AG said laughing as they reached the back door to the hotel.

With his man softening him up, Cash replied, "You're right Dog. I'm tripping, let's go smut these Bitches!"

THE SET UP

The girl's room was on the first floor, a couple doors from the back door exit from which they had come in. The door to the room was ajar when both men reached it. As Cash opened it all the way and walked in, Kim and Lisa were already down to their bra and were now removing what little they had on. AG shut and locked the door in a hurry, not taking his eyes off of the women.

"Y'all just gonna stare or are y'all gonna come hit this?" Lisa said, surprisingly loud while smacking her ass.

In the next split second before Cash and AG could react to Lisa's offer, two men with long pistols and in Ghost faces shot out of the bathroom. With pistols drawn and what seemed to be super-human speed, but to Cash it was happening in slow motion, the bigger of the two masked men smacked AG across the face with the pistol breaking his nose causing blood to gush out. Cash dropped automatically to his knees holding his hands up and the other masked man pushed him down aggressively on his face.

While getting hog tied, Cash yelled out, "You Trifling Ass Bitches, I'm going to kill you!" Before getting punched in the mouth and gagged.

Lana and Isis were dressed in seconds and already walking out of the room. Lana exhaled heavily as they walked briskly out of the back door of the hotel to a rental they had already parked out to the hotel.

When they reached the rented charger, Lana said, "Oh Shit Ice, I forgot my purse!" And was off running before Isis had gotten out a word to stop her.

Without thinking Lana slid the plastic door key down and up and pushed the door in. In the precious seconds, it took her mind to register what her eyes was seeing, she regretted ever meeting back up with her cousin X again. X had his mask raised to his brow and to Lana his face looked evil like a monster. He kneeled over a tied AG with his pistol in AG's mouth. Isis had just reached Lana and was tugging on her arm to shut the door so they could leave and get away from there. Isis wasn't looking in the room but heard the two muffled coughs and felt Lana's body tense up. X never realized that Lana was standing at the door until after he blew the back of the man's head off. Wiping splattered blood and bits of flesh from his face he noticed Lana out of the corner of his eye. As he turned towards her, they stared into each other's eyes. It seemed like they held each other gaze for an eternity before Isis pulled Lana away and shut the door.

Lana cried and cried as Isis drove them north on 13 heading toward Dover. After they got well passed Delmar Isis spoke.

"Lana, that don't happen all the time."

Lana yelled, "You knew that was going to happen?"

"No, I didn't but I know it does happen, and you shouldn't be so naïve, concerning what we do."

Lana still in tears cried out, "I can't do this anymore, I…I…"

Isis cut her off, "Lana, this is the fifth job you've been on and already got well over enough money for your whole college tuition. You got your own crib now, a newer ride, Bitch you winning! Five, six months ago you were flat broke and stressing."

"But I'm not a killer," Lana said.

"I'm not either, I don't think so anyway. If I was, I would have killed that Big Nigga's Ass myself. Blowing his stinking ass breath in my face all night." That at least got a smiled out of Lana. "I'm saying Lana; the end justifies the means."

"I don't want to go to jail Ice. X didn't have to kill them."

"Look, Lana, sometimes I guess it's too much money and drugs we take or rather X takes to let a person live."

"Like how much?" Lana asked.

"I don't know, a mill or two," she replied.

"Lana then asked herself, could she kill for a million dollars. Most people could," she thought.

Isis interrupted Lana's moral assessment, with a smile Isis asked, "Bitch what you thinking about?"

Staring out into the night with a blank expression Lana asked, "Could you do it Ice, kill for a million dollars?"

"Without hesitation," Isis spit out, "is water wet, or is the sky blue? A nigga can kiss da baby if he's the only thing in between me and that million." They both laughed for the rest of the ride to Lana's crib in Felton.

They talked about clothes, shoes, and the latest celebrity gossip. They talked about everything except what was on both of their minds… MILLIONS!!

CHAPTER 3

Walking to her car Lana couldn't keep the Kool-Aid smile off her face. She finished taking her last final and it was the first day of summer vacation. Lana passed her first year of college with flying colors and she was one step closer to a bachelor's degree in Business. Isis said she would take her to Secrets tonight to celebrate passing her first year, even though, neither of them was 21, but X had fake ID's made for them for when they were on jobs. Lana's phone rang as she was sliding into the back seat of her black Honda Accord (Black for her cousin X).

It was Isis, "Congratulations Girl!" she screamed and squealed in laughter.

"Thank you, Ice."

"Okay Lana, you have to go home, pack some clothes and come on out here to Ocean City now!"

"I thought we were going tonight," said Lana.

"Bitch, you know I had to rep for you. I got us a condo on the beach, hurry up so we can find our new boyfriends."

"Aww, that's so sweet of you,"

"Lana shut up and come on!"

"I'm coming, let me stop home and get my things. I'll call you when I'm close. Family with love, family with love."

When Lana got to the condo, she was surprised at all the people that were there, she called Isis for directions but Isis didn't mention it. X and the whole family was there. Kush, Lost, Hawk, Big Sexy, O.G., Doe from ROC and Starbuck. Even Lana's home girl Kisha was there. After everyone gave a toast to Lana, they all agreed to meet back to the condo at

8 or 9 to go to Secrets.

Everybody did their own thing, some left, and some stayed. Lana, Isis, and Kisha went together to the boardwalk enjoying the 85-degree day eating ice cream and talking. They stopped at Sunsations to get bikinis, sun hats, shades, and beach towels. Kisha insisted they stop to a bar before going to the beach. The first one they came across was the Purple Moose. Kisha ordered three daiquiris; strawberry, banana, and cherry.

They each took turns going to the restroom to change into their bikinis. Then each one of them gave their best catwalk as they walked back towards the others who whistled and clapped.

Kisha always direct and to the point stated, "When y'all gonna put a Bitch down? Y'all asses got cars, money, and on y'all way to owning homes and Shit. I'm still in a punk ass apartment. I thought we were girls!"

What she said took both Lana and Isis off guard. Because it seemed like it just came out of nowhere, but Kisha was dead serious. Lana spoke up, "Kish, it ain't like that, I wouldn't put you through the Bullshit and jeopardize your freedom."

Isis interrupted, "Let me speak to you for a second Lana, hold up Kish." Isis and Lana walked over and sat at a booth that was about 10 feet away. "I think we need to put her down Lana."

"Are you crazy, after what we seen happen last time, I don't even know if I want to be down!"

"Lana, you just like me, I just know for a fact that you been thinking of getting your hands on these millions you know are out there! I know I have!"

Isis was right, Lana's been racking her brain day and night about what she would have to do and how she would do it to get her hands on a million dollars. Her biggest question to herself was could she kill for it! Lana and Isis had gotten that fever that had touched many of men whether it was CEO's, athletes, movie stars, drug dealers, or stick girls. Money's the only quencher for the thirst they have and they won't stop until they count millions or die trying!! "Flawless diamonds, gated mansions, luxury cars, private jets, Versace, Gator, Jimmy Choo, Red Bottom, Hermes; Isis broke into millionaire dreams. If we plan on making million dollars moves, we gonna need Kish, matter fact we gonna need us a crew."

COLD CASE

In a small town in Southwestern Delaware, Detectives Andis and Way sat in a deserted bar called Stingers. Over Samuel Addams and Tequila, they went back over leads and wondered how nothing could have blossomed into a bust.

"A judge would say we have nothing but hearsay and he would never issue a warrant on what we have. We've been on this prick for freaking six months and can't catch him or his crew red handed or in the act of committing a crime."

Detective Andis paused to take a shot.

As he frowned, he spoke, "Your informant has to give us more! We need something BIG that's about to go down, cause Lords knows we're not gonna get a witness of any kind. These low life mutherfuckers I know are responsible for at least eight homicides this year, but with no witness..." He threw his hands up in the air without finishing his sentence, looking frustrated and at the end of his rope.

Detective Andis has been a state police officer for 15 years and Detective for 5 of those years. He seems to have aged more in the last year than all his years on the force. Andis knew personally who was behind his excessive drinking and all his pain in this last year.

Yusef Watson aka X. Detective Way, who was much younger than Andis, had only been on the force for five years and made detective. In his fourth year he looked up to and respected his elder but felt that his tactics were outdated up against these young gangsters. Way sipped his beer listening to Andis go on and on complaining, and how Chief Lynch would sooner or later demote them.

After hearing enough Way spoke up, "Andis we can't get this guy by staying in the guidelines of our rules and laws. We're gonna have to even out the playing field."

Andis blurted out, "What the Fuck are you talking about?"

"I'm talking about bending the rules and beating them in their own game. We need to be wolves in order to catch a pack of wolves! From what my informant has been saying these guys are smart, ruthless, highly cautious, and move as an organized network. We gotta find the weakest link in the chain and do any and everything imaginable in our power to bring fear and pain to them. That's the only way we'll see them to do what we need."

Andis, draining the last of his beer studs stood up saying, "Young man, if you and your informant can give me something worth going outside the guidelines of the law like you say. I'll think about risking my badge and pension, but it has to be something concrete that will put these bastards away for 3 life sentences! There's no way in Hell I'm gonna retire without taking this Punk off the streets."

DA CAVE

Isis whipped her black on black Lincoln LS in and out of traffic going at least 15 miles over the speed limit. Lana was gripping her armrest and Kish, in the backseat, was holding on tight to the leather straps about the door. Never noticing the fear of her two passengers, Isis explained where they were going.

"Why we going over Sister Vicky's crib?"

Lana heard X and all the crew talk about "Sista Vic" as they called her but she had never been there.

"Why are we going there?" Sista Vic is X's main safe house, cause that's where he keeps all his information about potential victims and marks.

Isis swung the Lincoln into an entrance of some project buildings Lana had never been before. Riding through at a snail's pace due to heavy traffic and cars parked on both sides of the street. Lana saw all kinds of people from toddlers to the elderly, hustlers to hard working honest law-abiding people out enjoying the beautiful day.

"Listen," Isis said, "Sista Vic is a very outspoken lady and we might get a little cussed out so don't take it personal, she talks Shit to everybody."

Parking in front of a 2-story tan building, Isis turned in her seat and looked at Kish, "I hope you didn't forget what I told you to get."

"Oh Naw, here I had forgot I had it." Kish handed Isis something in a plastic baggy.

Lana and Kish followed Isis down the packed sidewalk of dudes shouting out "cat calls" to them. Isis led them around to a side apartment of the adjoined units. Stopping in front of door 44, she took in a deep breath and exhaled before knocking. Lana noticed that Isis didn't just knock on the door with a regular knock but gave it something like a "drum roll" with both of her knuckles of her index fingers.

From inside came a high-pitched voice, "X you better not be playing with me."

The door was snatched open and an elderly lady with more gray than black in her hair stood in the doorway staring at Isis before she broke out in a grin, showing that she had a missing front tooth.

"What you want Ice? X ain't here," Sis. Vic said as she was walking back into her apartment.

Isis smiling like an innocent little girl said, "Sis. Vic, I came to see how you were doing."

That statement stopped Sis. Vic and she turned to the three girls and rolled her eyes, "I'm cooking me some steak, I ain't got time to be playing around. I know what you and X got goi…"

Isis cut Sis. Vic off, "I got some medicine for you Sis. Vic!" that shut her up but didn't take the scowl off her face.

"Who you done brought in my house, you know don't play with these Bitties out here, they steal."

"This is my girl Kish and this is Lana, X's cousin."

"You Big Austin's daughter ain't you?" Sis. Vic asked Lana. Lana was caught off guard and surprised. She hadn't heard her father's name spoken out loud in so many years.

"Yes, you knew my dad?"

Sis. Vic laughed, "Everybody knew Big Austin!"

Isis spoke up, "Sis. Vic, I wanna go in "Da Cave" and smoke some weed, I know you got some for me."

"Yeah, you know X left some here with me. Give me my medicine before you go over."

Isis told the girls to come on and she went to a mirror that was on the wall. It was about 6 feet from the middle of the wall and floor. Isis stood there for a second then turned around to Sis. Vic. Sis. Vic hit a light switch that was in the kitchen and the mirror swung open. Isis told Lana and Kish to go in as she walked toward Sis. Vic who held her hand out. Isis handed her the plastic bag what Kish had given her in the car.

"It better be good too, you know where the weed is," said Sis. Vic with a smile.

Isis went through the mirror and caught up with Lana and Kish who were in the middle of Da Cave just looking around. Isis smiled reading their minds.

"X put the lady who owns this apartment in a trailer in the country says he likes to be in the hood sometimes to humble himself."

One black leather chair and two loveseats set in the small living room, pictures of Scarface, Tupac, and Biggie hung on a wall of their own; this was X's cave. On the center of a black coffee table was a bowl of weed beside Don Divas and Old Source Magazines. Isis took a blunt out of her Ralph Lauren Bag emptied its guts on the table and fitted it with it lime green weed.

"Come on, let's go upstairs," Isis said as she led the way up and into a small room to the left.

The room didn't have much in it; four small chairs, a chalkboard, and some sort of glass table in the middle. Isis sat to the table and reached under it and hit a button. It lit up.

"This is an Idea Centre PC Table."

Lana and Kish simultaneously said, "What!"

"It's like a computer but in a table. X keeps all the information he gets in here about individuals hustling and soon to be victims. This is where he plans his attacks down to the last detail," while she talked Isis typed on a touchscreen keyboard. "Damn it, he changed the password," she said.

Kish lit the blunt that Isis had rolled blowing a sweet-smelling think cloud of smoke out of her mouth she asked, "So what are we gonna do now?"

Isis said, "I can figure it out, X has a one-track mind."

After about the fourth try she reached up taking the blunt out of Kish's mouth. Isis said, "I got it Bitch!"

Lana asked, "How did you get it so fast?"

"I just put in all the names of money that I've heard X say."

"So what was it?" Lana asked.

"What he says when he's taking somebodies money? Break bread." Lana and Isis laughed because they had heard him say that on more than one occasion during a robbery.

Lana was perplexed at all the information X had on these drug dealers. He was diligent in studying and doing his homework on each mark; he never handled any two the same. Names, addresses, what they sold, what blocks they were on, girls they were doing and much more. On some of the marks, X even had their birth date.

"Yo!" All three women heads snapped up at the same time at hearing the voice downstairs.

Isis dug in her bag and came out with a pen and small pad and showed it to Lana, "Write some shit down, I'm going down to stall 'em."

It was X, by now he was at the beginning of the stairs yelling up, "What y'all ladies doing?" Lana wrote as fast as she could, while Isis grabbed Kish and they hurried out the room down the steps.

Lana heard Isis say, "We were up here smoking, and showing Lana how to put this makeup on." Lana shook her head as she wrote thinking what a dumb alibi.

She switched the table off and ran into the bathroom and flushed the toilet and went downstairs. When she reached the last steps and turned into the living room she froze in her tracks. Isis was on her tiptoes kissing X. Now Lana always figured the two had something going on between them but she never asked.

"What up cuz, you miss me?" X said to Lana.

"No," Lana said smiling.

"Y'all nasty, we just came to see Sis. Vic."

X shook his head as he took a look at all three ladies, "Well, I'm glad y'all are here and..." Looking at Kish he continued, "by the look of it, Kish is part of the fam now. Cause Isis knows that nobody but family comes in here." All three of the women shook their heads in agreement.

"Alright," X said clapping his hands and then rubbing them together, "we've been on vacation to long, time to go back to work!"

CHAPTER 4

For the next three weeks, in Virginia Beach and Norfolk, X worked the girls harder and harder. Sometimes splitting them up to get a single dealer. X used the one vice that most men with money and power love; WOMEN. Not just any old women but sexy, pretty, young, Black women. The girls had so many different looks that X had to double take sometimes when he saw them after one of Lana's makeovers. They could go from looking highly sophisticated and sexy to outspoken, loose, and sleazy but still beautiful from one extreme to the other. Lana thought that some of the places X had them "bump" into a mark was pure luck and coincidental. That's until she started paying more attention to X. The more time spent around him Lana noticed he wasn't dumb. After the second week she knew X had these people lives down to a science and somehow, she was convinced that he had all this planned months ago. The last "stick up" Lana did in VA Beach was by far her easiest. *But as she thought about it, she came to the conclusion that the more stickups you do the easier they seem.*

X had rented a work van along with a Chevy Malibu as soon as they hit VA.

Isis and Kish were asleep when X woke up Lana at about 8:30 in the morning.

"Get dress, me and you have one more clown to hit. Wear something tight but simple like some workout spandex."

Lana drove the Malibu and followed X to a Belo grocery store. X pulled beside a Lexus IS F Sport, and Lana parked on the other side of X.

X called Lana's phone. "Hello, what are you hungry cuz?"

"No, I ain't hungry Girl, I told you what we're doing. Run in and get some orange juice or something. Look for this light-skinned wavy head fly boy. Flirt with him a little and beat him out of the store."

X pointed to the car on the other side of him, "That's his Lex, when you come out of the store, you'll have car trouble and when he comes to help, I'll take it from there. Okay?"

Lana, remembering everything shook her head, "OK, I got you cuz."

Lana thought as she entered the store and grabbed a handheld basket by the entrance, "This fool is crazy, it's broad daylight and we at the Belo's." She spotted her victim in the cereal aisle.

"Damn, X didn't lie, he sure is a pretty boy umm." *She thought as she walked towards him acting like she was searching for something.*

"Excuse me miss," the Fine Ass brother said, "I don't normally do this especially in the supermarket, but you're one Fine Ass woman. I would give you the world or die trying." Lana's heart fluttered but she had to remind herself what she was here for, but his light brown eyes had her in a trance.

After Lana gathers her wits she spoke with difficulty, "Thanks for the compliment but I bet you say that to all the women you see." She gave him a sexy smile and kept walking pass him. Before she reached the end of the aisle she saw him staring at her butt. "Maybe I'll see you around."

"Yes, you will most definitely see me," he replied.

Lana went to the checkout line to pay for her milk and juice and started to panic when she turned to see "Mr. Fine Ass" right behind her. *She didn't know what to do, X didn't exactly draw out a plan for her she thought.*

As the clerk rung up her items "Mr. Fine Ass" made his moves.

"Hi again, my name is Nice," he said as he extended his hand to her, Lana was stuck like a deer in headlights.

She shook her head a little because she was about to give her real name. "My name is Angie," while shaking his hand. He held her hand a little longer than necessary.

Lana paid the clerk and hit the automatic opening doors. Nice must didn't get much because he was right behind Lana as she went into the parking lot. Lana could feel Nice behind her, and knew he was trying to catch up to her without being too obvious. When she came into view of the Malibu, she smiled to herself and stopped in her tracks. Throwing her arms in the air she dropped them as if she was frustrated.

"Damn, a Fucking flat!" she said loudly as Nice was walking up behind her.

"Do you have a spare tire…Angie?"

"I don't know, it's a rental. You look like you're too pretty to change a tire," she said looking him up and down. She popped her trunk and he got the spare out.

"Looks can be deceiving Ms. Angie, I won't charge you nothing but lunch with me to change the tire," he said as he searched her trunk looking for something.

Lana said, "I need to see what kind of job you have first before I agree."

Suddenly out of nowhere, she heard X's voice, "Do you two need any help?"

Nice still looking in the truck said, "No not with changing the tire. But…would you happen to have a 4-way lug wrench?"

X opened the side door on the van saying, "Yeah, I should have one somewhere in here."

X got all the way in the van making noises like he was digging and searching for the lug wrench.

"Here you go Bro," he said as he stuck his hand out of the sliding door on the van.

Nice, talking to Angie with his mind on one thing, should have seen the signs or felt the vibes even if they were as subtle as they were. Reaching the open van door Nice brought his hand up reaching for the wrench. He didn't see the object pointed at him in X's other hand. X shot a two prong 1000-watt taser into Nice's chest and caught him as he shook and fell forward. Slamming the sliding door shut, X bound the man in gray duct tape. Lana stood frozen in the same spot not believing what just happened in a blink of her eyes. Knowing something is going to go down and seeing it go down are two very different things.

X jumped out of the van, threw Lana's spare tire in the trunk of the Malibu and said, "Drive next door to the 7-11 so I can put air in the tire."

Lana hopped behind the wheel and X followed her to the air pump. After he put air in the tire Lana thought her work was done and was about to head back and join the girls, but that wouldn't be happening anytime soon.

"Lana, I might need you to get this dudes bread."

Lana bawled up her face in protest, "I can't X, what if someone sees me?"

"You'll be alright; I've seen all that game you got. Just say you're his new girlfriend and smile," X said as he forced a smile, "let me talk to pretty boy and I'll give you the details. Follow me."

X drove about 10 minutes and turned on Monticello Blvd and into City Park. Lana followed him to the back of the parking lot shaded by huge oak trees. She parked beside the van wishing X would hop out and tell her that her job was done. Twenty minutes later X did hop out of the van sweating bullets.

Sitting next to Lana in the car he said, "Lana I do need you cuz." Lana just sighed. She wanted badly to be back in Delaware in her bed but…this was sort of her job.

"What do I have to do X?"

X smiled, "Imma take care of you cuz. This is all you have to do it's easy…"

NICE

Lana listened to the GPS as it stated that she has arrived at her destination. She pulled behind a gold Range Rover that was in front of the home at 1100 on 38 St. in Granby. Before she left the park, she changed into a floral dress by Michael Kors in the back seat of the Malibu and touched up her make and let her hair down. She took the Ralph Lauren collection bag that she had her dress in. As she opened the waist-high fence to follow the walkway, she admired the brick house that it led to. *The landscaping and rosebushes were beautiful, she thought.*

"Please, let no one be here Lord." Lana knocked and waited. No one came to the door.

She took the keys X had given her, looking around making sure no one was coming she opened the door. The front door opened to a gorgeous living room, what looked like antique cherry wood and soft beige leather.

When Lana realized her feet weren't moving and that she was just gawking around she said, "Let me get my ass out of here. In and out Lana!"

Now walking briskly through the house, she passed the first 2 doors to the bathroom and the master bedroom and went directly to the 3rd room. X had told her which room to go to, easing the door open she knew that she had the right room. A poster of Air Jordan gliding from the foul line looked down at Lana, along with a poster of the Virginia rap duo the Clipse. Lana shut the door silently and went straight for Nice's bed. X hadn't told her to get anything from under the mattress, but she checked because her dad always kept his money there. She was glad she checked; rolls of money were neatly placed from one end of the box spring to the other. Lana pushed the mattress all the way up to the wall with both hands and left it standing on the box spring against the wall. Taking her bag off her arm she rapidly raked all the rubber band knots into it. Then she spun around and went to the only window that was in the room. Bending down she peeled the carpet back exposing a rectangular metal box. Lana fumbled for the keys X had given her, on it was a big fat 4 prong key. She found it and drove it down into the opening of the safe that was planted in the floor.

"Oh Shit!! This pretty boy is rich!!!"

The safe was filled to the brim, but these bills weren't folded they were stacked. While looking around her hands continued to shake as she emptied the safe. As she stood, she didn't want to leave the mattress standing up so she tried to lower it with one arm while her other arm clutched the bag with the money. The mattress was too heavy to be brought down gently with one hand and it came down fast and hard making a loud "BOOM" as it thudded down on the box spring. Lana paused, not moving a muscle. Her heart pounded in her chest and then she heard what she was dreading.

"Gregory! Is that you Son?" Lana tried to hurry out the bedroom but ran smack into an elder lady eloquently dressed with all white hair.

"Child, who are you, and what are you doing in my house? Where's Gregory?"

Lana wanted to run as fast as she could but somehow managed to calm down enough to still her trembling body.

"I'm sorry ma'am, I'm Angela, Greg's new girlfriend. He sent me over to pick up some things for him." Lana wrung her hands together nervously waiting to see the old lady's reaction. The hawk-like eyes of the lady softens into barely being visible as she smiled showing pearly white teeth or dentures Lana thought.

"Oh, I'm so happy to see that Gregory has come to his senses and found a nice young lady like yourself instead of those fast butt hoochie mommas." Lana let out a relieved sigh as she followed Nice's or rather Gregory's mother into the kitchen.

"Are you hungry Honey? I'm about to cook some steak, eggs, and potatoes."

"No. Ma'am I have to get going, but I will be back later with Nice. I'm mean Gregory."

"Well, he should be here soon. He goes grocery shopping for me every other weekend."

"Oh, I forgot he said he would be a little later than normal in bringing your groceries. Is that lemon meringue pie?"

Lana called X as soon as she got back into the Malibu.

"Damn Girl, did you get it? Where are you? What in the world took you so long? I was about to run up in there shooting!"

Lana laughed, she had never heard X sound worried he was always so calm and smooth. Lana had stayed 30 more minutes talking to Nice's mother and eating pie. She liked his mother, *Lana thought, "Shame she would have made a nice mother in law."*

"I'm just leaving, everything is copasetic!"

"What? Speak English!"

"We good cuz, I got it."

"Okay good meet me at the park we were at earlier. Hurry please this whining ass nigga is plucking my nerves."

When Lana got to City Park, she spotted X walking with a book bag over his shoulder, he hopped in the car.

"Where's Nice?" Lana asked.

"I left him in the van."

"You didn't...kill him did you, X?"

"No! I didn't kill him but you worried about the wrong Shit!"

X noticed the look Lana gave him like she was frightened. "I left him alive in the van cuz, he's taped up but not too tight. He'll get up the nerve sooner or later to get out."

"Anyway!" he smacked his hands together and rubbed them like he was warming them up, "break bread!"

Lana smiled, reached into the back seat, pulled her bag out and gave it to X. X emptied the bag onto the floor and began counting. Lana had already taken 20 thousand off the top, which was all the money under the mattress. X sat up and leaned over and gave Lana a big kiss on the cheek.

"I love you Lanie and here, just like I promised," he said handing her a stack of money.

"What's this?" Lana said.

"A bonus, it's 25 thousand. And I still have to pay you your cut along with the girls which should be…"

X wrinkled up his face and counted on his fingers a couple of times before he said, "Another 30 or 40 thousand."

X continued, "Lana, I gave you that extra 25 racks because none of the other girls could have charmed the old moms like you."

Lana made a face like "whatever."

"Naw, I'm for real cuz, now if it was a nigga to seduce Isis could have done it with no question but it takes someone sincere to get a mother to let down her guard. Let's pick up the girls and get our asses back to DE."

SURVEILLANCE

"Excuse me Sir, but you'll have to remove your hood," a middle aged attractive Hispanic woman wearing a Belos Shirt and name tag said to Nice as he came through the grocery store doors followed by a large intimidating Black man with long dreadlocks. The ladies face contorted in shock as Nice removed his hood. His Versace shades did little to nothing to conceal his patch worked face.

"May I speak to a manager please?" Nice said to the woman who now was trying desperately to avoid looking up at his face.

"I'm the assistant manager, you can speak to me," said the Hispanic lady, now looking at Nice and the man with him that hovered close to Nice like an enormous shadow.

"Ma'am my car was stolen last week in your parking lot. I was wondering if I could have a look at your surveillance video to see if I recognized anyone involved."

Before Nice had even finished his sentence, the lady was shaking her head, "No sir. I don't think I can be any help to you. That's only available to staff, management or the authorities."

Nice dug into his pocket and pulled out a big wad of money, peeling off five bills, he said, "I not only think, but I know that we both could help each other out drastically. I'll give you five hundred dollars for last week's surveillance."

Looking around to see if anyone was close enough to hear the proposition being offered to her, satisfied the middle-aged Hispanic snatched the bills from Nice with the speed of lighting. "Follow me," was all she said.

SECRET ADMIRER

Two months after the crews VA campaign, Lana was well into her second year at Del State. Before school started, she took her mother shopping at Christiana Mall, Forman Mills, and then they ended up at King of Prussia. Lana gave her mother two tickets to the Bahamas and told her she had received them from her job and wanted her to go in her place since she didn't have time to go. Lana's mother was so happy; she had never been on vacation out of the country. She told Lana that she was the best daughter a mother could have. Lana smiled as her mother hugged her with tears of joy in her eyes for having such a special and successful daughter. Lana was just happy to be making her mother happy.

One-night Lana awoke in the middle of the night in a cold sweat. She had her second or was it her third, dream about making love to Nice.

"This is not good! I'm a 21-year-old virgin dreaming about someone I have no business even thinking about. I need a boyfriend or a hobby."

The very next day, X, Isis, and Kish surprised her by being outside Lana's car when she finished classes for the day.

"And what do I owe you all for to grace me with your presence?

"Hop in, I'm taking my favorite ladies shopping," X said getting back into his new SUV.

In his triple black Buick Anclar, X drove the ladies to the jewelry store Orly's in Wilmington. He brought all three women diamond earrings. He spent almost $9000. X got hugs and kisses from everyone.

Kish and Isis wanted to go clubbing but X said, "Lana's got homework and school tomorrow, let's take the party pooper back," winking at Lana.

When they dropped Lana off to her car she promised to go out with them the next night since it was Friday.

The next day Lana woke up energized and feeling good.

"Just three classes and my weekend will begin," she said smiling, thinking of the partying ahead.

Her last class of the day Language Arts was interrupted by a courier delivering roses to Lana. Surprise to her!! Lana was so embarrassed. She blushed as the whole class turned to watch her read the card.

From: Your Secret Admirer. You're the loveliest woman I've ever laid eyes on!

"Who could have sent this?" Lana questioned to herself.

She went to her mental rolodex of all the guys on campus that tried to talk to her. She quickly removed all of them from her search. Most of them were dogs and would think it's a waste of time and money to send a woman flowers. Regardless the roses still put a smile on her face and made her feel good that someone was thinking of her.

Driving home that Friday afternoon Lana was beaming from the roses being delivered and excited about her weekend, so excited that she didn't notice that a white Yukon made every turn she made. Pulling in her driveway she called Isis.

"What up Ice, where are we going tonight Girl?"

"Damn, you ready ain't you?" Isis replied laughing.

"Hell yeah, this schoolwork is killing me."

"X want to go to Philly."

While opening her front door, she cradled her cell phone with one shoulder while her book bag was on the other as she carried the roses. Lana felt a person presence behind her. Before she could turn around, she was pushed hard into the open door onto the floor inside. All Isis could make out before the call was disconnected was, "Bitch, I want my money!"

Trying to get up Lana was furiously kicked in the stomach by a hooded man.

"Help...Hel…" her screams were instantly cut off by a hand clenching her throat like a pair of vice grips.

"I'll break your neck Bitch if you try to scream again."

She was forced down on her back by the hand still gripping her neck.

The man ripped her blouse and bra off.

"Please, please don't do this. I'm a virg…"

Lana's pleas were cut off by the man pulling off his hood, revealing his face. She knew at that instant that her begging was in vain. It was Nice, but he wasn't the same pretty boy she had seen in the market. His face was scared up. To Lana, it looked like the jagged scar tissue formed in an X from his forehead to his chin. She gasped.

"Yeah Bitch, you like your friend's artwork?" Nice said as he turned his face from left to right while he's straddling Lana.

Nice seemed to rage even more as Lana looked at his face. He tore her pants off along with her panties.

"I'm going to teach you a lesson Bitch about taking what doesn't belong to you!"

He thrust into her as hard as he could and pounded and pounded. Harder and harder until Lana could fight no more. She just stared blankly crying towards the ceiling.

When police and paramedics arrived 20 minutes later, they found a duck taped, raped, and beaten Lana with a severed finger. All Lana could remember was Nice's final threat.

"Until your friend gives me my money back, I'm going to do this anytime I feel like it."

CHAPTER 5

The two detectives walked into the interrogation room and 6'4", 290 lbs., Anthony Cole lifted his hat off the table and sat back in his chair. Detective Way stood as his partner Andies sat, looking over papers that he bought in. Head still down going over the papers, Andies whistled.

"Looks like you'll be gray, old, and barely living when or if you max out this time!" Andies looking back at his partner, "this guy's been a habitual offender since years ago."

Big Sexy shaking his head stared into space.

"Mr. Cole!" Andies yelled, "I don't have to tell you that it's only one way that you won't see every last bit of 45 years or even 1 day in the pen! Son, nobody knows yet that you're in out custody with a gun charge. I want a certain individual and I know you can deliver him!" Andies lit a cigarette and gave it to Big Sexy trembling cuffed hand.

"45 years, you'll be almost 80 years old, if you live that long!"

Big Sexy with his eyes closed said, "If I cooperate, I go home now and the gun charge disappears?"

Andies nodded.

"Who…who do you want?"

"You know Yusef Watson aka X!!"

At the name Yusef Watson, Big Sexy knew who it was without the alias X, they were childhood friends! Tony or rather "Big Sexy" as he was called on the streets occasionally set dope boys and hustlers up for X. By being a bouncer at numerous clubs he comes in contact with plenty of victims from the surrounding states as well as Delaware.

Tony aka Anthony Cole was born and raised in a Seaford projects nicknamed "Da Bricks." That's were him and a young X became affiliated in the mid 90's. Hours ago Anthony was pulled over leaving Meadow Bridge, and in the engine of his 87 Black Monte Carlo police found an unregistered 45 automatic.

Before Tony left Seaford Police Department a deal was made. He had to set X up in any way he could, guns, drugs, robbery, or murder. No hearsay, the detective needed X with his hand in the cookie jar. They gave Tony one month to spring the trap and let him know that they would be waiting and watching.

PRESENT DAY

"X! X!" Lana called out in a raspy barely audible voice. She sounded hoarse and her mouth was dry as a desert.

X popped up and out of the recliner he was sleeping and rushed over to her. "Damn, I'm glad to see you up! I've been worried like crazy Lanie! I'm so sorry, this is all my fault for getting you involved in my lifestyle and for not killing that faggot."

Lana held up a hand in protest. Trying to speak, she massages her throat and tries to clear it. "Water," was all she could get out.

X left her room and was back in a minute with ice chips and water. Holding the cup and straw up for her, Lana's first gulp caused a spasm of coughs. She pulled on the straw until she emptied the cup of water and only ice remained.

"It's not your fault X. I'm grown and I made my own decisions. How long have I been in here?"

"Three days."

"X, you didn't call my mom, did you?" Lana said with a look of fear in her eyes.

"No, I didn't but if you didn't get up today, I was going to. Lanie, I'm going down there and make this mutherfucker wish I would've killed him the last time. You ain't got to worry about him or no one else cuz, I promise you!"

From the malice in the face and the tears in his eyes, Lana knew X was sincere. She felt the love he had for her. In a quiet voice to X Lana said, "I'm going with you."

"Nah! Nah Lana, I can't...I can't have that! I'm still responsible for..."

Lana shook her head and threw a hand up to X. Leaning in towards him she grimaced in pain before she spoke. Her whole body hurt and any little movement she made it hurt more.

"I am going down there with you and kill him myself! He raped me X!" Although she wasn't yelling X heard and felt every word. Looking at her it was like she was another person, X got goosebumps staring into her eyes. Dreadfully Lana said, "He cut my Fucking finger off too!" while holding up her bandaged right hand. "You or nobody else is going to stop me from killing him! Either you're with me or against me!"

X was nodding his head in agreement with her before she even finished her last words, "Okay cuz, I got you!"

Lana stayed in the hospital two more days before she left. Her aching body wasn't the only post-rape symptom she felt. Since the incident, she had nightmares about Nice and all the other hustlers she helped to rob. In the nightmares they all came, cutting, raping, shooting, and torturing her. Isis picked her up in a black Suburban with jet black window tints. They hugged for a good 5 minutes when Lana was in the huge SUV.

Both of them wiped tears away as they let go one another.

With tears still coming down her cheeks Isis said, "I called X as soon as your phone hung up…we were too far away…so I called the police. I'm sorry Lana, I love you. I'm…" Lana hugged Isis again.

"It's not your fault Ice, I know that's all you could have done."

Putting the truck in gear and pulling off Isis said, "We'll never live that far from each other again. We have to protect each other, you're my sister!"

Smiling Lana said, "With love?"

Isis responded, "With family love!"

Lana noticed they went past the turn off to get to her house and asked, "Where are we going Ice?"

"Oh, I thought you knew."

"Knew what?" Lana said back.

Looking pitiful, Isis said, "Lana we moved all the stuff out of your crib."

All Lana could say was, "Why?"

"You can't stay there anymore Girl. I put everything in a storage in Seaford."

Isis saw tears in Lana's eyes and a blank facial expression. She reached over and grabbed Lana's hand, "Lana, we have to get this sick Bastard! And we don't know how long it will take. You had to move!"

Lana wasn't thinking that far actually the reality of the situation was just now sinking in with her release from the hospital. Now thinking she didn't want to go back to that house and for the first time she realized her life would never be as it were before.

"X said for me to take you out to Sista Vic to Da Cave."

Lana had never stayed in the projects before even though Sista Vic's crib and Da Cave were laid out like and upscaled condo. No matter when she came to The Gardens, Lana saw that it was always people everywhere.

As Isis pulled around to where Sista Vic lived she informed Lana that Da Cave and Sista Vic's was always protected 24/7. Lana and Isis had to make like 4 trips through Sista Vic to move her things through the mirror that lead to Da Cave. Last, they hauled her 2 safes. After Isis helped her get settled in, she left and Lana rolled herself a blunt from X's stash.

Using her new Droid that Isis brought her she called a resort hotel in South Beach and made reservations in her mother's name. Her mother was still on vacation in the Bahamas but Lana didn't have any intentions on letting her come back home until she had her revenge and killed Nice. Afterwards, Lana called her mother and told her to get off in Miami and to enjoy herself until she could join her.

Her mother tried to protest about her job but Lana wasn't trying to hear it telling her mom, "Enjoy yourself on my expense you deserve it." Lana also called up to Del State and told school officials due to medical reasons she wouldn't be able to return for the rest of the year.

The next 3 weeks X put Lana through a sort of mini boot camp. To Lana's surprise, she now had a roommate. X had hired a personal trainer/self-defense coach for Lana and she would share Da Cave with him. 6'4" 270 lbs., "Stretch" was a muscular, light-skinned, baby-faced giant. He arrived on the same night she had and told her to be up and ready at 6 a.m. The first week was grueling. Lana, still hurting from being attacked and raped thought this dude was trying to kill her. If she wasn't running, she was doing calisthenics or punching a bag. At night, Stretch took her out to Concord to the shooting range and taught her how to shoot. Sista Vic laughed hard at seeing Lana barely able to walk from the workouts.

Even though Lana thought Stretch was cute, they barely spoke those first two weeks unless he was giving out commands or pushing her to do more. During the last of the three weeks, Lana and Stretch opened up to one another more with each passing minute. He didn't say anything straightforward to Lana, but she knew he wanted her, and she liked him too. After training for a week, they would smoke a blunt and sit and talk about everything imaginable.

On a Friday of the third week during their AM collectivities, Stretch informed Lana that that was their last day.

Lana not sure what he was talking about asked, "What do you mean, the last day?"

"X called me this morning and said my job is done. Just keep up the workouts and the running."

Lana didn't want to break the bond that had grown between her and Stretch. "So, will I see you again Stretch?"

"I would like to see a lot more of you Kalana."

"Me too, I mean I would like that too Stretch."

Lana was suddenly looking up into Stretches eyes, she couldn't recall ever getting up off the floor from doing her crunches. They embraced and Stretch gave Lana a kiss so passionately it took her breath. Lana's whole body tingled and was on fire. They released each other both looking anywhere else to avoid the others gaze.

"I...I...I think it's time for our run," Lana managed to say.

"Yes. Yes, it is," said Stretch.

When they walked into Sista Vic's after taking their jog, X was sitting at her table eating steak and eggs in his traditional all black. Between a mouth full of food, he said, "Be ready in an hour Lanie, we're going down South." All of a sudden, X stopped chewing and talking. He was looking from Lana to Stretch and then to Sista Vic. Smiling he said, "You right, Sista Vic." X dug in his pocket and gave Sista Vic a 20-dollar bill.

Sista Vic laughing loud now saying, "I told you!"

Lana with her face frowned up asked, "What she right about?"

X pointing at her and Stretch, "Y'all two, something's up! I can even see it!"

REVENGE

Heading South on 95, X was all business, no small or idle talk.

"My boys from Da Roc, Doe, and Shooter, went down Norfolk as soon as you were hospitalized. They had their eyes opened and been getting everything ready for us."

Lana asked, "Getting what ready?"

"Lana, you just didn't think we could go down there shoot the nigga in the head and come back, did you? Everything has to be planned and drew up, saves mistakes. And just because we gonna kill 'em, I don't see why we shouldn't benefit from his demise."

Lana looked like she was disgusted as she spoke. "So, that's what this is all about, you want to just rob him again! That's probably the only reason you're so in a hurry to go down there!"

X could see that Lana felt disrespected because she was yelling now. He had to pause and calm himself before he spoke so this didn't become a yelling match.

"Look, Lanie, I want this joker killed as much as you do! This is personal, so we gotta be sharp and use our heads, not our hearts, but we still gonna take advantage if the opportunity presents itself."

Now smiling X said, "And from what Doe and Shooter said, the opportunity just presented itself."

X and Lana met Doe and shooter at a small sleazy motel off of VA Beach Blvd called The Sunshine Inn. Lana had never seen Doe or Shooter but X assured her that they were brothers from Da Roc and loyal. As soon as Lana walked into the motel room the variety of guns on the mattress reminded her that she just wasn't setting dealers up to get robbed anymore. Along with knives, ammo, and a couple pair of brass knuckles the mattress didn't have an empty space on it. Seeing that everyone was in the "gorilla suit" as X called it, Lana took the duffle of gear to the bathroom so she could change. Lana had never felt this nervous in her life, she looked at her pinky finger that was now a nub to encourage her to do what she had to do.

While changing, she heard Shooter briefing X on what he knew.

"Your man Nice never leaves the company of one or two of his goons nowadays," Shooter said smiling revealing two gold fronts, "I had to front like a junkie and cop like five times before I could pinpoint their moves and tail them. Nice rides with Goon 1 and 2 everywhere, picking up money and dropping off work all day. I picked one spot that's the most convenient for us because it's not in the heart of the city and it's like a straight shot towards our way home. It's in Ingleside it's an older dudes crib. I don't know if it's his pops or just his OG. I assume its money there because it's not a lot of traffic and Nice only hits there every other night or so."

Lana came out of the bathroom in an all-black bodysuit with butter Timbs on just as Shooter was finishing up. All three of the men looked at her and gave her an approving nod of her "gorilla suit."

She guessed X noticed her nervousness because he passed her the blunt, he was smoking saying, "This will help."

Now Doe spoke, "It took about a week of watching the house before she came back, but like you said…"

X cut him off smiling as he finished Doe's sentence, "Old women just can't leave their homes, even if it's not safe there."

Doe continued, "After that, it was a piece of cake. Nice put his moms in a townhouse off of Newtown Road with one bodyguard."

X asked, "Doe just in case we get some work out of this crib did you already set up a buyer? You know we can't ride all the way home dirty like that."

"Yeah I got a nigga name Herc from Accomack County, he will meet us when we get back over the bridge."

X looked Doe in the eye and asked him, "Do you trust him?"

Doe replied, "I trust him enough to buy dope or coke at a bargain price, who wouldn't?"

X smile and gave him some dap. Lana took a 9mm with a silencer off the bed along with a bowie knife in a sheath. Popping the clip out of the gun, inspecting the ammo and inserting it again, she caught a glimpse of herself in the mirror on the wall. Looking at herself in the mirror now she realized how calm she looked and felt. *"That weed X passed me must be doing the trick,"* Lana said to herself.

"That's what you rolling with Baby girl?" Doe said motioning towards the 9 she held, "I Fucks with them too." Doe held up his 9 with a silencer.

Lana said, "Well, this is the only gun I've trained with."

X speaking loud said, "Alright y'all let's make this Shit happen! Remember, this time, we're leaving no witnesses!"

As Doe and Shouter walked out of the motel room X called Lana back.

"Lanie, you sure you wanna roll? We would think no less of you if you wanted to chill here until we're through."

Looking intensely at Lana, X waited for her answer. Hesitating Lana took her eyes off her Timbs and stared back up into X's eyes.

"On my dead father's soul, I'm killing Nice tonight!"

X smiled and turned to lead her out the door. He didn't tell her that she had just given him chills with the conviction in her voice and that look she gave him like she was staring deep into his soul. He had no doubt that she meant what she said. It was already agreed that Lana and Doe would go to Nice's moms while X and Shooter went to the stash house in Ingleside. Lana liked Doe's personality already, even in this tense situation he was so relaxed, and like X still found humor and time to joke.

Turning down what he called his "ride out music," which was DMX's first cd, Doe's one gold tooth flashed as he talked. "Baby girl the mom's house is on a cul-de-sac in between two other townhouses. I just thought of a little something to get us in there." It only took them 15 min to get to the development.

"Alright Baby girl," Doe said, "drop me off right here. Remember what I told you, take your time."

"Gotcha," Lana said.

Lana drove on slow, pushing down on the brake every 20 or 30 seconds making the car jerk. As she came up on the cul-de-sac, she hit the brakes more rapidly and harder making her head thrash forward and backward. Lana stopped the car and popped the hood in between two of the townhouses along the curve. Instantly when she got out of the car she spotted the silhouette of a large man smoking. She saw the red cherry and then she smelled the sweet aroma of some good green.

Lifting the hood up she noticed Nice's goon already coming towards her.

"Yo, you got to move this car!" The goon said still walking toward her but about 50 feet away.

Lana's heart pumping now, wondered, "Where the Hell is Doe?" to herself, but out loud she tried to use her sweetest voice, "I don't know what's wrong Sir, it never did this before."

20 feet and closing fast the goon spit out, "Look Bitch you got one minute to get this piece of Shit out…"

He abruptly stopped talking in mid-sentence just before reaching the hood where Lana stood. Doe's pistol was at the back of the goons' head. Taking the goons gun from his waistband, Doe stuck the big man's gun on his own waist.

"Get the Fuck in the car Nigga before I pop your Ass," Doe said opening the back door and pushing the big man in and sliding in after him, all the while still holding his gun steady on the man.

Lana closed the hood and hopped in under the wheel and backed the car up into Nice's mom driveway.

"Who's the Bitch now?" Lana said looking in the back seat at the big goon with her 9mm pointed at him too.

"Look Homie," Doe said tapping the barrel of the silencer against the goon's temple making the goon take his eyes off Lana.

"I'll shoot your Ass and somebody will find you stinking in this trunk! Do you want to live?"

The big man nodded slowly.

"Alright, where's your phone?"

The big goon went for his phone clipped to his belt.

"Put your Fucking hands back up! If you move again, I swear I'll put a hole in your head!" Doe snatched the phone from the goon's belt and gave it to Lana.

"OK, you're gonna call your boss. That nigga Nice and making it sound mad convincing because your life is depending on it. Tell 'em his moms fell and broke her leg."

Lana frowned giving Doe a pleading look and said, "A broken leg?"

Doe replied looking at Lana, "You got a better story?"

Turning back to the goon who was now sweating, profusely and shaking uncontrollably Lana said, "Say she's having a seizure or something and he needs to get over here right away!"

Doe taking the phone from Lana gave it to Nice's big goon. "If you don't give an Oscar winning performance, you're dead!"

Lana and Doe listened as Nice's phone rang. "Yo, what up?"

"Nice, you gotta come quick! Your mom's having a seizure or

something man!"

"What!! Make sure she don't swallow her tongue…I'm coming!"

Lana did a silent clap, smiling at the goon and said, "Yea, you did excellent and the seizure guess was good too!"

Doe rolled his eyes and snatched the phone from the goon. "Time to go see what mom's cooking," Doe said.

Lana walked a little behind Doe as he marched behind the goon with his pistol in the big man's back. As soon as they crossed the threshold to the townhouse the aroma of fried fish hit their noses. Doe and Lana followed the goon through the living room toward the kitchen where they heard a Charlie Wilson song playing. Just before they reached the kitchen, they heard a woman's voice over the music.

"What took you so long Reggie? After I feed you sugar, are you gonna make an old lady feel like she's 19 again?"

Lana suppressed a laugh while Doe was in the front of her shaking his head. Simultaneously with entering the kitchen Doe shoved Reggie hard. Before Reggie could regain his footing, Lana heard two muffled shots from Doe's silenced weapon. Nice's mom holding a plate of fish and potatoes gasp in horror and looks terrified as she dropped the plastic plate and spun around from the stove taking in the shocking display. Then Nice's mom tore her gaze away from Reggie's lifeless body up to Lana's eyes.

"You! You Jezebel!" Doe grabbed the old lady by the arm and sat her down at her table in the kitchen.

"Don't move moms or I'll do you just like I did your young stud," Doe said.

Taking his phone out, Doe called X, "Yo we in, that nigga should be here in 10 to 15 minutes. Y'all coming?"

Listening to Doe speak to X, Lana noticed Nice's mom was now glaring at her ranting away. The old lady stopped only to shake her head as if she was disgusted by Lana.

"Boy never listens…I told him to kill your Ass! But he did bring me back a souvenir," the old lady said while holding up her pinky finger and wiggling it. Lana couldn't believe the words coming out of this sweet old lady.

"He said you enjoyed it too…when he…when he," a satanic smile grew on the old lady's face, "when he took you and…"

Without even thinking or hesitating, Lana was on the old lady with a fist full of gray hair firing shots from her pistol into the lady's face. After releasing the old lady's hair, what was left of her face made a wet sounding thud as it smacked into the table.

"I was just about to do that!" Doe said bringing Lana's attention back to him instead of watching her watching the old lady's corpse.

Wiping splattered blood and bits of flesh from her face Lana continued listening to Doe as he said, "X and Shooter ain't gonna be here no time soon, we gonna have to take care of ole boy by ourselves."

In a calm and motionless flat tone, Lana said, "He's mine don't touch him, I'm killing Nice myself."

"Alright Baby girl, I feel you. Come on let's get ready he'll be here anytime now."

MEANWHILE

In a two-story Ingleside apartment, X stood over a bloody-faced bald-headed man, whose chin was in his chest. X had already broken a couple of the man's fingers with pliers. The same pliers he used to twist and yank three teeth out of the man's mouth. But to avail the man just grunted and scowled in pain but wouldn't give X the satisfaction to see him even yell outlet alone beg for mercy. Getting frustrated due to the time they were consuming, X told Shooter to search the house. Running down the stairs 15 minutes later Shooter called out, "I got it! I know where it's at!"

X's immediate response to Shooter's news was to pull out his pistol and, "PHF, PHF, PHF." X put two shots into the bald-headed man's chest and watched as it heaved and deflated his last breath. X followed Shooter back up the stairs while Shooter explained how he knew where "whatever" Nice was hiding was at.

"I looked in this closet," Shooter opened the closet showing X, "and I noticed this spatula and drywall putty, along with this paint."

"AND Nigga?" X said anxiously.

Shooter looked at him smiling, "You ain't too bright, are you?"

Pulling a hammer out of the toolbox in the closet Shooter headed towards the bathroom explaining, "The paint in the closet was green and the only room in this apartment that's green is the bathroom."

The bathroom was small and cramped with the two of them in there. Their eyes searched frantically any and everywhere for clues of a secret compartment. It wasn't until X shut the door that both men said "BINGO" simultaneously. On the wall, a sign read *A fool and his money shall depart!!"*

Shooter started banging holes in the wall and started pulling off the drywall. X helped with his hands. It wasn't until they had destroyed almost all of the drywall on that wall that they were able to see a deep shelf from the ceiling to the floor. It looked like rows of cinder blocks wrapped in plastic on almost every shelf. Taking his hands with some difficulty X ripped the hard plastic revealing evenly stacked bills.

"That's what the Fuck I'm talking about!" X yelled as the two men embraced and were all smiles. They quickly started to pull down the blocks of money.

REVENGE PT 2

Nice burst into the townhouse wide-eyed and looking worried. Not until he was 5 steps beyond the threshold that he heard the door slam shut behind him. Spinning around his eyes bulged as he saw the two figures on each side of the doorway he had just stepped through.

Double taking at the sight of Lana, Nice attempted to speak but before he could Lana had fired a compressed shot from her silenced 9mm into his thigh.

Grappling his wounded thigh with both hands Nice yelled out, "You Bitch!!"

Lana fired another shot into his other thigh and he collapsed on the floor screaming in agony. Doe and Lana dragged Nice into the kitchen where he let out a groan in grief at seeing his mother slumped dead at the table. As they duck taped him to a chair tears streamed down his face as he called out for his "Mommy" until finally, Lana taped his mouth shut. Laying her pistol on the table, Lana unsheathed her knife.

Bending down Lana whispered into Nice's ear, "I've been dreaming of this moment, Nice."

She gripped Nice's jaws. Forcefully, pushing his head back so he was staring at the ceiling. Lana dug the point of the knife into the healed scars that formed an "X" on Nice's face, reopening the old wounds.

"How the Hell did you find me?"

Lana yelled, then snatching the tape from Nice's mouth. He didn't speak, Nice just clenched his jaws tight looking like he was grinding his teeth and started menacing up at Lana. Lana, without warning, stabbed her knife inside the bullet wound on Nice's left thigh. Nice howled in pain as Doe standing a few feet away grimaced but didn't take his eyes off the action. Removing the knifepoint from his bullet wound Lana asked again.

"How did you find me?" Gasping for breath like he was drowning with his whole face glistening from blood and sweat.

Nice stuttered and sputtered until finally he mustered out, "Sur... Surveillance from the store I...I'm so...sorry."

Before the last word was out of his mouth Lana heard someone "gasp" in the back of them at the entrance of the kitchen. Seeing Doe out of her peripheral spinning around a split second before she attempted to herself. But before she turned 360, she heard and felt all through her body a deafening "BOOM, BOOM." Lana saw Doe go down then she scooped her 9mm off of the kitchen table just before driving behind a counter that formed and island.

Lana heard Nice yelling, "What in the Fuck took you so long to come in…yo, kill that Bitch!"

Just then Lana remembered Doe and Shooter saying that Nice didn't move unless he had one or two goons with him. She felt stupid and ashamed for letting that vital information slip her mind, all because of her rage for Nice. An ear-splitting shot was fired at her as bits and pieces of wood and ceramic rained on her. Lana crawled along the island putting as much space as she could between her and the gunman. She didn't know exactly where he was and was afraid to peek over the counter to take a look. Then she heard Nice ordering the gunman.

"Come cut this tape off me! Hurry that crazy Bitch shot me!"

Lana heard a high-pitched ring as Nice's goon snatched a butcher's knife from the knife rack she had seen on the counter.

Suddenly she heard Nice screaming, "Yo, Yo, watch out he's not dead."

In the next fraction of a second in Lana's mind's eye, she saw Doe raising a weary arm aiming his pistol at Nice's goon. She knew that this was her only chance and that she and to do something.

Springing up from behind the counter Lana screamed while she fired; "Mutherfucker," PF PF, PF, PF catching a heavy set brown skinned man with long dreads in his neck and chest. The dread head stayed on his feet for a couple of seconds clutching his throat. His instantly blood-soaked shirt rose and fell rapidly as he tried desperately to catch his breath before crashing to the floor; dead.

Lana ran over to Doe, hopping over the dead dread head before kneeling down to him grabbing his hand. Doe had a silly grin on his face flashing his gold tooth. He had taken a hit almost directly in the center of his chest, and from the size of the hole, Lana knew Doe wouldn't make it.

In a weak, raspy, and labored voice he said, "Baby girl…Baby girl…we got…to…burn…da place."

He was gone before he could finish, his dead eyes staring at Lana. Lana stood, looking down at Doe with an emotionless blank face, and then directed her cold unnerving gaze to Nice, who had been quiet since his dreaded gunman was killed. Nice was silently praying that the madness and chaos had been too much for Lana and that she just ran away leaving him behind and alive. But seeing that haunting dead stare, he knew that his prayers weren't answered.

Lana walked slowly over to Nice only stopping to pick up the roll of gray duct tape that was lying in a pool of blood. Nice, now pleaded for his life. "I'm so sorry. I'll give you millions if you let me live; please, please, please don't…"

Lana put tape over his mouth and secured it by wrapping it around his head three times. Looking down on Nice she unsheathed her knife, never removing her sinister stare from his eyes. After reaching down unbuttoning his pants she slashed and tore the jeans until they were shreds lying around his ankles exposing his thighs and groin.

"You still want me Nice? You don't have to take it! But that's how you want it right? You want to rape me?" Lana spoke in an unusually calm voice as she stroked his penis gently.

Nice mumbled inaudibly shaking his head hard and fast.

In one gracefully smooth motion Lana pulled hard on Nice's penis with her left hand and without a pause, the knife in her right hand sliced off his manhood.

Nice screamed and screamed behind the tape as he tried with all his might to break lose and get up, but he struggled in vain. Lana continued to stare at him until he took his final breath and his heart stopped pumping blood out of his wounds.

Thirty minutes later Lana was jolted out of a stupor by a hand touching her shoulder. It was X looking around the kitchen with a puzzled expression on his face. His lips were moving but Lana didn't hear anything nor did she comprehend what was going on. Not until a whole minute of watching X's mouth move and his now frighteningly expression did Lana come back to her wits and heard X saying, "Are you alright? What the Fuck happened?"

As he looked down at Doe while his hand squeezed both of her shoulders. It seemed that X's touch opened up a floodgate of emotions in Lana that for hours she had held in check. She gripped X tightly in a bear hug crying uncontrollably.

"It's alright cuz. But let's get the Fuck out of here! Shooter, take Doe in the back yard and then burn this Bitch down!"

X lead Lana outside to the car, him and Shooter came in and stuffed her in the back seat. She sat there pressed against the door by bulky trash bags filled with something solid.

A couple of minutes later Shooter hopped into the car and X squealed wheels peeling away from the now a blazed townhouse.

CHAPTER 6

X awoke from his dream praying that it wasn't reality. He heard Lana's name escaping his mouth as he opened his eyes. X had another nightmare of a blood-soaked Lana, this time killing him. In the four months since Nice's murder and X's 2.3 million dollars come up, he had these sort of dreams constantly. After giving Lana her cut of over half million dollars, which he had to insist that she take, X told her to bank her money and he brought her a house. A four-bedroom ranch home deep in the country of Greenwood on five acres of land; most of it fenced for horses. He also paid for Lana and Isis to go on vacation to Hawaii and told them to stay as long as they liked. X felt guilty for bringing Lana into his lifestyle and for her pain she suffered. No matter how much money he spent on her he couldn't shake the feelings of remorse for her. He knew after seeing what she had done to Nice and his mother, plus the expressionless look on her face that she would never be the same mentality again.

On coming back from VA, X let Lil D handle everything concerning heist, he just sat back and took his cut once a month for being the boss, but last week, wanting to get away from his own thoughts of guilt and remorse, he told Lil D that he was riding with him on the next job. Lil D informed X that the next job's inside man was his old friend Anthony, "Big Sexy" Cole. It was 3 o'clock before X got dressed and left to meet Lil D over at Da Cave to go over a plan for Big Sexy's mark. When X stepped through the mirror into Da Cave, he heard Lil D talking on his cell phone.

"I don't know if we can do it tonight."

Seeing X come in Lil D passed him the phone, "Yo! X...X, you have to do that thing tonight, homeboy's shipping everything out tomorrow."

X signed before he spoke, "I thought the nigga wasn't going to re-up until the day after tomorrow, and you said it would be only bread!"

"Yeah, I know what the plan was," said Big Sexy, "but the nigga copped out yesterday for some reason. He's moving out for Cali in the morning. Nothing else has changed except that instead of cash it'll be about 20 birds."

X was quiet for a moment contemplating what Big Sexy just said. He never rushed into a heist and even though his gut feeling was saying, "Fuck this job," X was still silently weighing his options.

Lil D was sure X would tell Big Sexy no because X had never let an inside man dictate his moves.

Lil D was shocked when X said, "Alright, but your cut just got smaller!"

Ending the call X looked up to Lil D and said, "Tonight's the night Dog!"

X and Lil D watched for any moments at the tan double-wide with brown shutters in Bethel, De. After a short time of lying down in the dirt observing the house from a wooded area across the street, a pearl white CL-A Benz pulled up. A white dude with a ponytail hopped out of the driver's seat and skipped over to the other side of the car to open the door for a short, dark-skinned woman with an hour glass figure. X heard faint laughs as the couple walked arm and arm to the double wide. According to Big Sexy, the white dude was Joey Knuckles, supposedly Nicky Scarfo's cousin from out west. X and Lil D waited exactly 20 minutes for the couple to get nice and comfortable before they made their way to the front door with pistols in hand. X held up one finger, then two, and then three before kicking in the door with his butter Timbs. As usual Lil D crossed the threshold first moving fast and low, but before X could take a full step into the house, he saw a burst of light and heard a nerve shattering BOOM.

Lil D was thrown back into X by a shotgun blast to the chest. Attempting to drag Lil D to the side of the house for cover from the gunfire, the distinguished sound of an assault rifle cut loose on him. Jumping to the ground sideways so that they weren't in front of the door, X felt Lil D's body release its last breath and lay limp in his arms.

With so many shots coming his way, X couldn't even return fire. Lil D's lifeless body took hit after hit lifting it off the ground. X sprinted in between falling and crawling to the same woods that he and Lil D were just at, scoping out the house.

Just as he reached the cover of the woods he heard sirens and saw red and blue lights reflecting off of the trees. Not stopping to look back, X tripped, fell, and ran until he got to the other side of the woods where he had parked the squatter.

He hated leaving Lil D's body behind, and it wasn't until he reached the car and drove off that he realized the burning sensation in his left arm.

BREAKING NEWS

BREAKING NEWS

An all-points bulletin is out on a Sussex County man by the name of Yusef Watson. Considered armed and dangerous, Watson is wanted for the murder of Delany Tillmen. If anyone has any information on Watson's whereabouts, contact Delaware State Police. <u>A REWARD IS</u>

<u>BEING OFFERED</u>!!!

THE TAKEOVER

Isis and Lana were having the time of their lives in Hawaii. Lana felt so relaxed and carefree. Their days and nights consisted of shopping, going to the beach, and clubbing. Isis wanted so badly to ask Lana what happened in VA but knowing deep down that Lana had killed stopped her from being nosy. She figured Lana would tell her when she was ready but having never killed before, Isis was anxious for every last detail. Isis did notice that Lana was now willing to drink more liquor and smoke more weed than she usually did. Lana even took an "E" pill a couple of times since they've been in Hawaii, something she had never done before.

On more than one occasion Isis had to call Lana repeatedly to get her attention after she'd zone out and stare at nothing in the middle of a conversation they were having. When these such behaviors happened, Isis justified to herself that that was Lana's way of coping with her past dramatic events.

One day lying on the beach both of them in sun hats and shades, reading romance novels, Isis said, "Let's buy a house out here Lana, it's so perfect here."

"How much money do you have Ice?"

Isis was taken so off guard by the quick change of conversation and the directness of Lana's question that she couldn't respond; she sat looking puzzled.

"I'm just saying Ice; I consider us sisters and what's mines is yours."

Lana now making eye contact with Isis said, "Ice... I have well over half a million dollars."

Isis' mouth fell open, she assumed that Lana had more money than her but she never thought that much more. They had dreamed of making millions together. At last Lana saw what she was looking for, a genuine smile from her sister saying that she was truly happy for her.

Finding her tongue, Isis said, "Damn Girl you've been putting in work!" But the compliment didn't bring a smile to Lana's face, actually, Isis thought Lana grimaced.

Isis continued, "I have about 250 racks," she said looking at the Pacific Ocean to avoid Lana's eyes.

Lana put a hand on Isis's shoulder for her to look her way, "I'm going to make sure we reach that million together Ice, but until then, what's mine is yours!"

"Thank you, Lana," Isis said with a big smile. Seeing her friend so happy wiped the grim expression off Lana's face and she smiled too.

As Isis flirted with a local Hawaiian dude favoring The Rock by the edge of the tide as Lana continued to read her romance novel.

Her phone ringing interrupted her, "Hello?"

"Queen Bee?"

"Kush?"

Kush was the only person on earth to ever call Lana Queen Bee. Other than speaking to him when she saw him with X a couple of times she had never seen or spoken to him other than those times, and he had never called her. His deep baritone voice and tone didn't sound friendly to her when she heard "Queen Bee."

"Yes."

"X has been hurt."

"What! What happened?"

Kush ignored her question. "I need you to come home."

Lana responded, "Alright, we're on our way now!"

Kush replied, "Call me at this number before you land so I can have someone to pick you up at the airport."

"Okay!"

"With family love," Kush said.

Lana repeated, "Family love."

Before arriving at BWI two days later Lana phoned Kush a couple hours ahead of time like he told her. From the time Kush told her X had been hurt her imagination took off in a million directions. She pictured X on his death bed riddled with bullet holes gasping, desperately holding onto life. Anxiousness kept her awake most of the flight back east. Isis continued to ask questions that Lana didn't have the answers to, and eventually cried herself to sleep.

Lana and Isis were met at baggage claims by a tall brown-skinned man with dreadlocks past his shoulders holding a sign saying *"Queen B."* He greeted them with a warm smile saying his name was Hawk and that he would take them to Kush.

After taking their luggage, Hawk lead them outside to an Audi A8. Isis and Lana smoked some purple haze that Hawk gave them as he drove. They rode for about two hours before stopping outside a massive wrought iron gate. Lana had recognized the area as Rehoboth Beach. The gates were opened electronically and Hawk went through them driving down a long winding lane. Lana didn't know if the big house that they were getting closer and closer to was Kush's or not, but she was, and could tell that Isis was, in awe at the enormity of the estate.

Stopping in front of the mansion Hawk jumped out of the A8 and opened the back door so Lana and Isis could get out. Kush stood in the huge doorway waiting for them to climb the pyramid shaped steps. When they reached the top, he embraced them both then turned to lead them into the house. With an arm over each women's shoulder, he guided Lana and Isis down the marble floors and artifact filled hallways.

"X is alright," Kush finally said, "he was shot, but it wasn't anything life threaten." Kush thought he felt tension and stress melt away as both women shoulders relaxed. "But unfortunately, he's in a situation with "da Jakes. He'll be on the run until we can clear this matter up."

Isis and Lana just listened quietly, they had already heard and seen the police reports on the news and radio. They knew X didn't kill Lil D, it just had to be some misunderstanding.

"Oh, I'm sorry Ladies," Kush said, "did you enjoy your trip?"

Simultaneously both women said, "Yes."

"Good, cause y'all have work to do."

Before Lana could question him on what he meant by the statement, they stopped at the entrance of a huge room. The room looked like some sort of library with about 50 or 60 people in it, milling around. The majority were Black males but Lana did see some females here and they were doing various things.

"Isis, you'll have to wait here while Lana comes with me."

Isis wanted to protest badly but she knew from X that sometimes orders were meant to be followed without question. Isis just nodded and stepped into the room and found a seat on a leather couch across from two men playing chess.

Taking Lana's hand Kush continued to lead her through the enormous mansion.

"Lana, did X ever go into detail on…why he does what he do?"

For some reason to Lana, Kush didn't seem comfortable talking about robbing.

Lana said, "You mean robbing people?"

"No, but I assure it's for the money," sounding sarcastic.

He seemed to not notice the sarcasm as he responded, "Well, that's what we're here for Lana, to clarify and get some things in order."

Stopping and turning to face Lana, with a smile Kush said, "Just remember I have your back and not to worry X is my best friend."

He turned and opened a pair of French doors that Lana hadn't even noticed. The doors blended with the mahogany color of the wall. The room and everything in it were white. The rectangular shaped room had a huge round table in the middle. The other side of the room, from which Lana and Kush had entered, was all glass, facing out towards the ocean. The view was breathtaking. Lana didn't take her eyes away until one of the two men that were sitting at the huge round table when she came in walked over to her.

A tall brown-skinned man with corn rows took Lana's hand with a smile and said, "You must be Lana, da Queen Bee. I'm Sizzle." He led her to the table and pulled a chair out for her to sit in.

As he took his seat, Sizzle pointing to the man sitting across from Lana, "And that there is Ice Bezzel." The man Sizzle pointed to was a short muscular man with a caesar haircut and a beard.

Icy Bezel nodded n Lana's direction but didn't look too happy at the present moment to Lana. When Kush found his seat the four of them sat in silence. Lana watched Kush and Sizzle roll blunts from a large bowl of weed in the center of the table while Icy Bezel glared at her puffing on his black and mild. Lana sat anxiously waiting for someone to speak.

She thought to herself, "Why am I here? They could have told me over the phone that X was ok."

With his blunt pearled and sticking out the side of his mouth Kush spoke while lighting his green.

"Queen Bee, I know you're wondering why in the Hell you're here." He paused, after getting the blunt lit to inhale deeply, "We three are the head of the family, along with X, but X is now…at the present time…uh on hiatus. With not being able to do what he does best for the family, he has appointed you to fulfill the family's obligations…in your chosen…profession."

Lana took the blunt when Sizzle passed it to her and hit it hard, coughing, she managed to say, "What!"

She couldn't believe what she was hearing. She stared at the three men through the haze of smoke as Kush, sounding like a corporate CEO gave her a company promotion. Lana almost laughed out loud at the thought of Kush being a corporate CEO because from the looks of it that's exactly what they were.

All three men wore expensive suits. Lana had recognized their brands on the first look of each man. Kush wore a Dolce & Gabbana suit with John Lobb shoes, Sizzle an Emporio Armani with Tom Ford shoes, and Icy Bezel wore Gucci everything. Sizzle speaking brought Lana out of her daze at admiring their clothes. Realizing that she was super high from the weed she passed Sizzle back the blunt.

"Queen Bee," he continued, "X chose you and we," motioning to the two other men at the table, "have to abide by his call. That's one of the rules we all agreed to when we formed the Family, no matter who disagrees with X appointing you."

Lana noticed that when Sizzle said those last remarks that he cut his eyes towards Icy Bezel and Icy returned with a smirk. Lana took the blunt that Kush passed to her reluctantly as he spoke.

"We, along with you now control the flow of coke, heroin, and weed on the Eastern Shore. Sizzle controls everything that has anything to do with Chronic from midgrade to the best Shit on earth. Bezzle, the H, from manufacturing to distribution to retail and wholesale. I handle all coke, soft or hard, keys to balls. And your part is to take product and money from who we refer you to…or…in some occasions to just remove the person or people."

Lana heard a loud sigh come from Icy Bezel she knew he didn't approve of her taking X's place. She figured he didn't think she was capable of doing the jobs that the position required. *"I'll show him why X appointed me to take his spot,"* Lana said to herself while she grits her teeth and shot Icy Bezel her most furious look.

Lana had no idea that when X and Ice said, "Family Love" to her that they were talking about an East Coast Mafia, she had always thought that they were just talking about the bond the three of them shared.

Icy Bezel slid a manila folder across the table to her. He stood blowing smoke from his nostrils as he fiddled with a scarf that was draped around his neck.

"That is your next job, in there you'll find information in your next mark, and what must be done."

Looking at Kush and Sizzle he said, "This will definitely prove to us if X made a rational decision by appointing her."

Now turning to look at Lana, Icy said, "Cause I don't think you can handle this burden. Look at you, you're too pretty and soft…"

"ALRIGHT!!" Lana had enough.

"Mr. Icy, we'll just have to see if I'm up to the job." Lana gave him her most seductive smile, "How about we put a small wager on it?"

Icy Bezel returned her smile, "50 G's."

HAPPY BIRTHDAY

A black Benz Limo hit the corner of 39th and Market at a snail's crawl. Immediately the driver had to stop because of the line of cars that was blocking the street. Minutes later a short chubby Dominican man wearing a red, gold, and blue Versace shirt with cream pants and blue loafers motioned with two fingers for the Limo driver to pull up to where he was. Waiting for the tinted window to come down, the Versace-clad man stared at his reflection until slowly the window came down. Revealing a tall light-skinned baby-faced man with glasses wearing a chauffeur's suit with matching cap.

"Hello, could you by any chance point me in the direction of a…" The driver looked down to a card he was holding as he read.

"A…Jesus Inglaz?" The chubby man wearing the Versace snatched the card out of the driver's hand.

The card was from a company called Adversity ENT specializing in

Adult Parties with Jesus Inglaz's name under recipient. After looking over the card for a few seconds the Versace don directed the Limo driver to pull over so the cars behind it could go pass. The Versace don approached the Limo driver again after the driver had parked.

Leaning down with broken English he asked, "Who sent you?"

The driver said, "Sir it's against company policy to…"

But the chubby Versace-clad man interrupted, "Why you come look for da boss?"

Feeling frustration, the driver lets out a sigh, then leaned toward the Versace wearing man and whispered, "It's his birthday! There…there're presents for him in the back!"

The driver waved the man to come closer, the chubby Dominican leaned in with his head halfway into the Limo driver's window. The driver hit a button and the private wall between the front and the back of the Limo started to go down. When the wall finally came all the way down the chubby Dominican let out a hearty belly shaking laugh at the sight.

Sticking two of his fingers into his mouth the chubby man whistled and a boy who looked about 13 or 14 that was sitting on a crate ran over. After speaking rapidly in Spanish, the boy then ran off into the bodega on the corner. While the Limo driver waited, he tried with all his power to look calm, a steady stream of traffic poured through the block. He knew all the traffic in cars and the sick looking people walking pass wanted one thing and one thing only; Heroin!

Stretches nerves were starting to get the best of him, he was seriously wishing that he didn't agree to go on this mission with Lana. He had never done anything besides work a 9 to 5. Stretch had to admit to himself that he being head over heels for Lana is what had gotten him into this peculiar "job." And "job" was the key word, Stretch would get a big payoff plus be around to protect and watch over Lana. When Lana propositioned him with being the fourth and only male of her hit squad, Stretch thought, the robbing and sometimes killing that the job required was a bit too much for him. On further thought, he had been training in martial arts, boxing, and wrestling all his life.

Stretch said to himself, "I might as well get rich for something I love to do!" Now that all of what he had planned for with Lana and Isis for this last month was actually happening, he felt like puking from anxiousness, anticipation, and his adrenaline racing through his body. After waiting for what seemed like an eternity but was actually about five minutes, two Dominican men walked out of the bodega where the boy had run into. The one guy that led the way was short and muscular with tattoos over all the parts of his body that his tight wife beater didn't cover, even on his bald head.

Stretch immediately recognized this man as Pepe, Jesus bodyguard. Pepe's picture was in the portfolio that Lana had him study, detailing the objectives of the job. Stretch also noticed Pep's gun bulge that was covered by his beater and tucked into his tan Dickies as he walked. The man following was no doubt Jesus Inglaz. With the air of royalty, he was slimmer and taller than Pepe and look like he stepped out from between the pages of GQ. Wearing a dark blue Hugo Boss Suit with matching Prada Frames, he smiled as the chubby man pointed to the Limo while they walked towards it.

Pepe reached Stretch's window first immediately drawing his pistol pointing it at Stretch.

Stretch, scared but still sticking to his script, reached for the sky. "I don't have any money; I'm just working…"

Jesus yelled something in Spanish then Pepe reluctantly tucked the pistol back into his waistline.

"It's OK Pepe," Jesus said to his bodyguard with a sly grin on his face as he opened the back door to the Limo.

"Happy Birthday papi" was all that was heard over all the activities going on around them in the streets said by what sounded like the most, loveliest women on Earth.

LAY LOW

In the South West corner of Delaware, dead on the Maryland-Delaware line, sat a white bungalow with black shutters. In this small house deep on a deserted back road was Anthony Cruz aka "Big Sexy" who was and has been in hiding for the last three months. Detectives Andies and Way put him up out here in the middle of nowhere with the hopes that they would have caught X sooner, but due to the delay in X's apprehension "Big Sexy" was on pins and needles fearing that X would track him down and kill him, especially after what the detectives just did. Andies and Way were kicking in every door were X ever hung out at and frequently harassed all his known associates.

The last raid they authorized was to Vickie Springs, aka Sista Vic. She wasn't arrested but Big Sexy was definitely worried because he had given the detectives Sista Vic's apartment number, praying the detectives found and killed X, but instead of finding X the detective trashed and broke everything in Sista Vic's crib, in the process, kicking the mirrored door and discovering the entrance to Da Cave.

After confiscating X's computer table, the detectives. Interrogation of Sista Vic's ended up with her being hospitalized.

"You broke Sista's Vic's arm, X's gonna KILL ALL of us," Big Sexy said looking worried and like he hadn't had a peaceful sleep in weeks.

"Nonsense, we're cops," Detective Way said with a smirk pointing to himself and Detective Andres. "Now, you may be in big trouble with your big homie X," Way said talking to "Big Sexy."

Andies interjected, "If you didn't have us protecting you, but we'll have his Ass soon enough," he said while making a mock gun with his hand, making pretend he was pulling the trigger.

It didn't take much more of the detective telling him to stay, and his thoughts of X torturing him, that finally, Big Sexy agreed to stay hide.

But Big Sexy thought to himself, "These mutherfucking cops think this is a joke, X gonna for sure put bullets in these pigs for touching Sista Vic, and me too for doing the unspeakable."

The detectives had brought Big Sexy an ounce of sour diesel because he wanted to get high and they wanted him to stay put.

"Give us another week Anthony and I swear we'll have him. With your testimony, he's doing life and you can go on with your miserable excuse of a life. Alive and free," said Detective Andies on his way out the door, "you know the procedure, no company and don't tell anyone where you're at!"

Big Sexy staring off into his own world managed to reply with a barely audible, "OK," under his breath. *He was wondering how his life had gotten so Fucked up, so fast.*

After the detectives were out of the door, Big Sexy picked up his phone and dialed a number, thinking to himself, "Fuck that, I need me a shot, haven't had any in almost a month."

"What up Sexy?"

"Yeah, this me. You gonna let me play in that wet wet or what? We've been talking on this phone for weeks; I'm trying to make this official tonight Evita."

"Alright, I'll text you the directions."

Big Sexy had called Evita a petite, caramel complexion women with short hair. They met at the yearly AFRAM festival held in Seaford, DE a few months ago and have been talking on the phone ever since. Their meeting was genuine and Evita, honestly felt a connection with Anthony aka Big Sexy until her cousin Rita filled her in on what's up with Big Sexy. Little did Big Sexy know, they had more in common than a sexual attraction.

SURPRISE

Pepe's guarded and protective demeanor didn't diminish with the sight of the lovely, yet scant dressed woman. Jesus held the Limo's door open with pleasure for his bodyguard to assess the situation. Jesus smiled at how Pepe always took every precaution there was to take in protecting him, even with inspecting these beautiful harmless women. The three women had completely different looks and complexions but all three looked like goddesses to Jesus. They were wearing lingerie that revealed just enough to make a man's imagination run wild, concealed only by an equally stunning silky and more sheer seductive looking robes. Each woman wore different colored lingerie and robes complimented by matching stilettos and large hairpins that held all of their hair up deliciously displaying their throat and nape. The three of them moved hypnotic but with a purpose as soon as Pepe's and Jesus' back hit their seats.

Lana and Kish were on each side of Jesus tugging, unbuttoning, and trying to remove his clothes. They were aggressively kissing, sucking, and licking his neck, face, ears, and chest. Pepe stared down with untrusting eyes as Isis kneeling between his legs raised his wife beater and placed soft kisses on his tattooed stomach and chest. His emotionless, stone cold face didn't give any hint that he was aroused, but Isis felt the bulge rise up and press against her stomach. Suddenly without a warning Pepe pushing Isis aside leaned over and banged on the partition.

Stretch lowered it just halfway before Pepe spoke, in surprisingly excellent English, "Drive one street over to the Dominican Café."

Lana had already drawn it up in her plan that Pepe being Jesus security would prefer another place to bed them if she and her girls passed Pepe's threat assessment.

Taking them to a secluded area let Lana know that Pepe had fell for their disguises and their acting, which for the most part was, staying calm, cool, and collect. The other parts were acting promiscuous, looking sexy, and keeping a "yes man" attitude. Although Lana's exterior appeared as if she was enjoying a party, inside she had butterflies and her mind was racing a hundred miles an hour. She was searching for the perfect time to unleash terror on her mark.

Pepe was a problem, the girls all agreed that he should be taking out first or kill the both of them at the same time. Lana got chills when Pepe looked her way with his soulless eyes, they reminded her of a snake's eyes. At the thought of a snake's eyes, Lana's mind rewound to a couple of weeks before when she found herself face to face with one of the world's most poisonous snakes, the Taipan.

When this job came up, due to Lana and the girls' harms to get close to the Dominicans without having any visible weapons on them, she had an idea. Lana contacted an old high school friend that loved lethal and poisonous animals, Robbie Elison. Come to find out, now he ran an illicit black-market ring of exotic animals.

In a secluded area outside of Bethney sat high-tech state of the art facility in disguise as old faded red barn in the back of Robbie's house. Lana looked on flinching as Robbie handled the deadly snake carelessly and with ease as he extracted the venom. After placing the taipan carefully back into its large tank, Robbie held up a clear container about the size of a small cup. Holding it up high so Lana could get a good look at the yellowish fluid, Robbie Elison spoke, "Just saying, hypothetically," as he held up the quotation, "that you wanted to kill a man. It wouldn't take no more than couple milliliters, so you have well over enough. But that's just speaking…"

Lana blurted out, "I know hypothetically."

Lana paid Robbie a generous sum of $20,000 and said that she might use his expertise in the future. He said that his door was opened to her anytime before she left his headquarters.

"Senorita, Senorita!" Jesus distinctive voice broke Lara's thoughts.

They were in front of the Dominican Café and Pepe was outside holding the Limo's door open for them.

"Come!" Jesus said holding out his hand for her.

Lana gave her hand to him but not before she made eye contact with her two friends to assure them that it was about to be "show time."

Outside of the Limo the street and sidewalks were bustling with people of all shades of colors and professions. Jesus led the three provocatively dressed women towards the café, but he didn't go into the entrance. Jesus went to a door to the left of the entrance that opened a staircase going up. Standing to the side he directed the women to go up while he and Pepe brought up the rear. Once all three women were at the top of the floor, they had to stop because it was too dark to see anything.

Lana heard a loud smack and then felt Jesus or Pepe's powerful hands around her neck. Suddenly a blinding light was switched on and Lana saw that it was Jesus standing over her as she fought desperately for her breath, clawing at his huge hands. Lana didn't want to show off her martial arts or self-defense skills just yet, she figured she could endure this assault and wait until the time was perfect.

After what seem like a lifetime of being without air, Jesus released Lana. She fell to the floor coughing trying to catch her breath. When Lana's lungs were working like normal her sense of awareness shot back up. She immediately noticed that Kish was lying on the floor beside her and that Pepe and Jesus were strapping Isis in some contraption. Focusing on her surroundings, Lana saw that the room they were in was coated with red plastic on the floor, ceiling, and walls. The room had all kinds of contraptions made of chains and leather. With a quick gaze, she saw whips, spikes, cuffs, and even small rodents in cages. Lana's calculations only took seconds before her mind registered that they were in a sadistic freaks dungeon and if she didn't do something fast, they would probably die right here.

Isis fought Pepe and Jesus while they were trying to strap her down to a table that would have her lying down spread eagle. Lana scooted over to comfort Kish who was bleeding from a head wound. Lana figured Pepe had smacked Kish with his pistol.

"Are you alright?" Lana whispered.

Kish replied by shaking her head. Lana's only other words were, "Get ready."

Pepe pulled his pistol back out and pointed it at Isis. "If you don't stop, I'll shoot you and then still Fuck you!"

Isis stopped resisting and let Jesus strap her down onto the table. With Isis fully strapped down to the spread-eagle table by her wrist and ankles, Jesus and Pepe step back to observe their catch.

Looking over towards Lana and Kish with his gun down by his side, Pepe threw his head back and gave a high-pitched cackle. Lana watched his Adam's apple move up and down. Just before she rolled on her left shoulder in the direction of Pepe. Simultaneously with rolling Lana attempted to remove her hairpins from her hair and sprang up into Pepe. In slow motions, Lana saw herself in her mind eye snatching her razor-sharp hairpins that she had coated with the taipan's venom that she had purchased out of her silky hair. Reality sped up for her when she leaped air born seeing Pepe raising his chrome pistol.

Plunging the poisoned hair pins into Pepe's neck, blood squirted and sprayed Lana from his pierced jugular. Pepe's eyes bulged not believing what just happened while his trigger finger squeezed uncontrollably from pain and shock, firing all around the room.

Isis watched helplessly as Lana stabbed Pepe and dove for cover behind a wooden contraption that would have its occupant bolted down on all fours. Isis could do nothing but pray that one of Pepe's bullets didn't hit her.

She prayed out loud Psalms 23. *"The Lord is my shepherd; I shall not want. He makes me lie down in green pastures..."*

Kish, still on the floor when Lana made her move went after Jesus, who wore a sadistic smile on his face until he saw blood gushing out of Pepe's throat. Trying to make a run for it, Jesus was stopped short of the door by Kish wrapping her arms around his legs from her position on the floor. Jesus went down fast and hard to the plastic covered red flooring, banging his head. Kish pounced upon his midsection before he could react, yanking both of her deadly hairpins out of her hair in one fist.

With her free hand, Kish struggled to hold Jesus down while at the same time raising the poison-dipped pens and her clenched fist. Jesus cringed in fear shutting his eyes with the anticipation of the pain coming, only to never feel it. Kish's forceful downward thrust was interrupted by a massive jolt that shook her body and slowed the momentum of her fatal blow. Her body tensed up and then relaxed as she fell on top of Jesus. One of Pepe's bullets had hit Kish in her back.

Lana froze in her tracks at the dreadful image of Kish's lifeless looking body sprawled on top of Jesus. Rage filled Lana and her body reacted without a single thought telling it to move. Lana pried the pistol from Pepe's death grip just as Jesus was pushing Kish off of him. Both of them rose to a standing position simultaneously and for a split second which seemed like an eternity, they made eye contact with each other from across the room. Lana pointed the pistol at Jesus her movements were steady and deliberate.

Jesus pleaded by throwing his hands up in front of him, palms facing Lana saying, "Por favor mama, por favor!"

Lana squeezed the trigger without flinching or blinking, "Click, Click, Click, Click." Seeing that the gun was empty, Jesus charged at Lana like an angry bull and within five long strides he crashed into her. Landing on top of Lana with all his weight Jesus knocked the wind out of her lungs stunning Lana momentarily.

Infuriated, Jesus punched Lana in her face repeatedly. Then he wrapped his hands around her neck and squeezed.

"You Bitch!" he hissed with a strained voice while applying pressure.

Lana tried and tried to break from Jesus' vice-like hands but grew weaker and weaker up against the madman's strength.

Lana's vision blurred and then started to fade. She thought a miracle had happened seconds later while coughing air into her lungs when she was just so close to death. But it was no miracle.

Once Lana caught her breath along with her wits, she realized Jesus was lying beside her twitching in a pool of blood. Isis stood over him watching him gasping for his last breaths. Lana saw one of the poison-dipped hairpins sticking out of Jesus' chest and the other one out of his neck. Lana closed her eyes and asked for forgiveness from the Lord. She knew the job had to be done but she felt regret because she allowed Isis to take a life. She knew Isis would have nightmares now, just like herself.

CHAPTER 7

X wore a two-button wool and Mohair Suit by Salvatore Ferragamo, cotton shirt by Ermenegildo Zegnaj, cotton and silk tie by Thomas Pink, glasses by Prada, leather shoes by Brioni with a Ferdora by Louis Vuitton, all in his signature…black.

He looked like the many other business executives or politicians in attendance tonight at the HBCU's annual conference in Washington D.C. Many prominent alumni to black colleges addressed the politicians and businessman on the importance of the black school.

Like Lana, X had attended Del. State for a couple years but never finished. He donated every year to the HBCU's fund during the event, and at this time he always reflected on his life, second guessing his motives and means. During the last year, his life had taken dramatic turn after dramatic turn.

After he was shot and Lil' D killed, X spent months recovering from being wounded physically and emotionally. Dr. Kadiesha "The Families" doctor tended to X at her lavish home tucked in the boondocks outside of Bridgeville. She was diligent with not letting him leave until he was completely healed physically. It was voted on and agreed, that once he was in good health by the other founding fathers of "The Family," to keep X's successor in place until the matters concerning the cops and Big Sexy were handled. X agreed, but reluctantly.

He knew Lana was capable of handling anything that was thrown her way, but X didn't want her soul or conscience to be the price on account of him. X's team put the word out in the street that anyone with information about the whereabouts of Big Sexy would get a hefty sum.

Not wanting to stick around DE because he was wanted by the police, but also not wanting to be too far away in case someone call with a tip about Big Sexy, X stayed in the North East, going to the surrounding states and cities; New York, New Jersey, Boston, Baltimore, and now D.C.

He felt burnt out, bored, and lonely with traveling, new faces, and even meeting different women. After hearing what Detectives Andes and Way did to Sista Vic, Kush had to fly out to X personally to talk him out of going back to DE on a war path. Therefore, for a week the two best friends tore into the City of Baltimore's clubs and hot spots just like old times.

With the bad news about Sista Vic came the two names of the detectives to X. He just knew they were behind killing Lil D and framing him. He swore to Kush before he departed back to DE that he would kill them and clear his name. Last week, X received the phone call that he had been waiting months for but from a strange and unusual source.

As he sipped his champagne, his thoughts drifted to the unsuspecting phone call.

"Hello?"

"How are you handsome?" came the reply from a sweet-sounding voice.

"Who's this?" X spat.

"You cannot go on forgetting about your future bride."

"Evita! How you doing Sexy?" X said with a legitimate smile.

Once every two or three years, X and Evita always seemed to make it back to one another for a couple of passion filled days rekindling an old love.

"Yusef! I was so worried about you after I heard what happened to

Yo…"

X interrupted, "I'm alright Ev, it wasn't bad as you probably heard. Anyway, when can I see you?"

"Hold up, let me finish what I was saying."

"I know what you called for, you miss me and…"

"Yusef! I do miss you but I have something for you...I've been talkin to Anthony."

The silence from X after hearing Big Sexy's name out of the mouth of one of the few people he loved spoke volumes to Evita.

Knowing some of the thoughts he was thinking, Evita spoke fast, "I didn't Fuck 'em Yusef!"

"Where? Where is he?"

"Ha-ha, ha-ha!" Evita's laughter sounded innocent, but X knew she was capable of malicious acts to get her way. She was amused by the fact that she had something X wanted so badly. She said flirtatiously, "I hope you're this anxious every time you hear my voice."

"Evita, this ain't no joke. Tell me where he is!"

"Yusef, as soon as I know exactly where he is, you will be the first to know. Give me a week or two and be ready. OK?"

"OK"

"But Yusef, before I give you what you want, you have to promise me you'll give me what I want."

"I promise," X replied without hesitation.

X grimaced at that thought as he took another sip from his glass of champagne. His mind was a million miles away from the beautifully dressed women and well-mannered men that he was in the company of. X shared a table with a middle age black male with a Ph.D. in medicine from Howard and two Black women each with degrees from Grambling. The current speaker held the attention of everyone at the gathering. X studied each of the people at his table and wondered what his life would have been like if he had remained in college and had not pledged his life to crime. *"I surely wouldn't have to dodge bullets," he said to himself.* He was wealthy but at a drop of a dime, he knew his life could be turned upside down. "I guess it is time to come clean on my promise to Evita, this is the third time I made it."

Just as everyone in the auditorium stood to their feet and begin to applaud to the speakers closing words, X's phone vibrated.

"Hello, HOLD ON I CAN'T HEAR YOU." X walked toward the exit of the huge room.

"Yusef! I know where he is, how long will it take you to meet me at the Woodland Ferry?" Evita said so anxiously that X heard her Spanish accent.

BACK AT THE CAFÉ

Back in front of the Dominican Café, Stretch had to block the doorway from two guys going up to where the girls were. The two Dominicans must have heard the gunshots that Stretch had heard and was attempting to check on their boss.

The smaller of the two Dominicans pulled out a 9millimeter. He threatened Stretch without saying a word, by motioning with his pistol for him to move. Froze with his hands raised to the sky, Stretch prayed for a distraction or diversion. Stretched got what he wished for seconds later, when Isis and Lana burst through the door carrying a bloodied Kish in between them. The armed man's double take at the women was just enough of a hesitation that Stretch needed.

With lightning quick speed Stretch closed the gap between him and the men in one giant step and with a massive overhand right, struck the gun welding man on the temple. Before he could follow up with his left the small Dominican was crumbling to the ground and the 9millimeter flew from his hand.

Lana dropped Kish's arm to retrieve the discarded pistol. The other Dominican attacked Stretch by jumping onto his back, trying to choke him. Lana tried but couldn't get a clear shot of the man who was getting bucked and spun around. Stretch's body was too huge and powerful for the medium built Dominican man. He pulled the man's entire body clean over his head and within seconds Stretch's strong hands had snapped the man's neck.

Throwing the limp body to the ground Stretch turned his attention to the women. He snatched up Kish into his arms like she weighed nothing at all and rushed her to the Limo. Isis jumped into the driver seat as Lana, Stretch and Kish got into the back. Glass shattered and rained down on them in the back seat as automatic gunfire rang out behind the Limo.

Squealing wheels, Isis hoped the curb fleeing from the gun shots and dodging people on the sidewalk. After hitting a couple vendors selling hot dogs, fresh fruit, and water ice she fished tailed the Limo out into the street blending in with the flow of traffic.

BIG SEXY

A few hours after his last phone call, Big Sexy, playing his John Madden game, was interrupted by a knock at the door. Jumping up with a big grin on his face, he already had a boner in anticipation of this booty call. Looking down at his hard on, he chuckled, then closed his robe over his wife beater and boxers as he strode to the door. Since he had spoken to the lovely Evita earlier, Big Sexy had downed almost a whole pint-sized bottle of Crown Royal and smoked a couple blunts of sour diesel. Stopping just for a second to steady himself against a wall, he shook his head to clear the grogginess and continued to the door with only a slight wobble.

He unlocked the two dead bolts and pulled the door open with a little too much force from drunken energy. Big Sexy pissed himself instantly as he stared into the holes of a sawed-off double-barreled shotgun. At the other end of the shottie was X with a sinister smile on his face.

Big Sexy attempted to speak but only an inaudible whimper came out, "I...I'm...I'm sorry X."

X jabbed him across the bridge of his nose with the barrels of the shottie. Big Sexy stumbled backward, eyes growing to the size of saucers with the thought of getting shot in the face. He fell to the hardwood floor with shock written all over his face. Swiftly, X stepped into the house closing the door behind him.

X's first impulse was to blow Big Sexy's head clean off his body. That's the only reason he had the shottie in tow. Nothing would have made him feel better right now than to see Big Sexy's blood spill, but calmer head prevails. On the drive over X felt that he had a plan that would kill three rats in one trap. Reeling in his anger and rage, X kicked Big Sexy savagely in his gut and stomped his already bloodied face until the man just laid there crying, covering his head and face in a fetus position. X's grim baritone cut through the air with ease and rang in Big Sexy's ears like chimes.

X's voice oozed with malice, pain, and hostility, "You're gonna die today, in this house! But...before you go...Imma give you the opportunity to die with a small piece of dignity."

ISIS AND KISH

Miraculously the bullet went straight through Kish's shoulder without hitting bone or artery. Lana applied pressure on the wound until she and the crew switched vehicles. In the van that Stretch had stashed for them a few blocks away; it had a change of clothes and a first aid kit that he used to stitch up Kish's wound. Lana made the call to Kush, informing him that the job was done. He told her to come straight to the mansion.

The hour ride to Rehoboth began in silence and was full of tension. Stretch comforted Kish in the back while Isis drove and Lana rode shotgun. The act of murdering Jesus Kept reoccurring over and over in her mind as Isis drove. The scenes got more graphic and the details sharper as the act ended and began again.

"ICE!" Lana called out from the passenger seat. "ICE!" she yelled louder, "slow down Girl!"

Isis snapped out of the trance she was in and took her foot off the accelerator.

Lana gently grabbed Isis's arm, "Are you alright?" Isis wiped perspiration from her brow.

"Yes, I'm sorry Sis...I need some green in my life," Isis said giving Lana a quirky smile.

"I know me too," Lana replied as she pressed her head against the headrest and pulled the lever on the side of the seat, so she could lay back.

"Are you alright, though, Ice?" Isis felt Lana's eyes on her as she tried to focus on the road and heard the concern in her friend's voice.

Yes, I'm good Girl; you know X got your girl, right?"

"I know that's right!" Lana said. Suddenly both women were all smiles with the mention of X.

"Do you remember that fool made pretend he was our gay friend so we could get the Gtown dude?" Lana said laughing.

"Yeeesss Girl," Isis said in between giggles, "he was so mad that he had to act like a faggot that we had to stop him from killing the dude before he told us where the stuff was." They both laughed so hard that they were in tears and their stomachs ached.

The gates opened automatically without them having to speak into the intercom and they proceeded down the long winding lane to the mansion.

"I miss him Lana, and I know you do too," Isis said. They held hands to comfort each other.

BACK AT BIG SEXY'S

X towered over a bloodied and terrified Big Sexy, who sat duct taped to a wooden kitchen chair. Smoking Big Sexy's sour diesel, X blew smoke down into his face.

"Now, are you positive that both of them Dirty Ass Cops are coming here tomorrow?" X asked.

Big sexy shook his head making sweat and blood fly, trying to talk through the tape covering his mouth.

"Good, they gonna pay for what they did to Lil D!" X snatched the gray tape from Big Sexy's mouth so hard and fast that it took off a patch of his facial hair but Big Sexy could care less, he was worried about his life.

X put the blunt to Big Sexy's mouth. Big Sexy took a long and deep pull off the blunt, never taking his eyes off of X.

"X! X! I had no choice! Don't kill me...please don't...Mmm Mmm…"

Before Big Sexy could say more, X reapplied the duct tape. X sat in a chair that positioned the kitchen table between him and Big Sexy. X didn't say another word, he just continued to puff on the sour d and stared at Big Sexy. Big Sexy couldn't meet X's intense ice grill, he closed his eyes. After over an hour of silence, there was a drum roll like knock at the door. Big Sexy's eyes popped wide open and darted from side to side nervously.

"I ain't gonna kill you, Anthony," X stated as he rose from his seat and walked out of the kitchen towards the front door.

A couple seconds later X reappeared followed by a skinny light-skinned older man with bug eyes carrying a duffel bag. Big Sexy trembled even more than he already has been with the sight of the older gentleman.

Between slow exhaling and deep inhaling X said, "Anthony, he's gonna kill you! I trust you heard of my man Boneyard!"

The man known as Boneyard grinned at the expression on Big Sexy's face when his name was spoken. His grinned revealed that he was missing his two front teeth. Boneyard's name was always mentioned in stories along with words such as gruesome, horrific, and torture. Not too many knew what he looked like because most of those who were introduced to him, he executed.

X patted Boneyard on his back and said, "Keep an eye on my old friend while I make a call. No need to rush, we've got plenty of time before those pigs come."

As X walked into the living room, he stuck his head back into the kitchen and said, "Oh and get Big Sexy's phone and text them pigs something that will have their thirsty Asses running over here."

Boneyard just gave a nod as he unzipped his duffel bag that he had placed on the kitchen table.

CHAPTER 8

"Hola beba como lute y amas."

"Hola Roberto!"

"Hola JuJu, mi amigo said that everyone will be there when you all arrive."

"De acuerdo, we leaving now, we be there in an hour, don't worry about nothing, I'll handle everything just the way you like Boss, those bastards will pay for what they did to Pepe and your brother Jesus!"

"Escuchar JuJu, our friend says make for certain you kill all in the photos you have," Roberto said sternly.

"OK!" JuJu answered, "call you when the job is done."

Roberto ended the call and immediately texted his friend that he was referring to JuJu about. That friend was currently inside The Family's mansion. "ENROUTE." Was the only word that he texted and the one-word reply was, "EXCELLENT!"

Roberto "EL OSO" Inglez, is the boss of the Dominican Cartel. EL OSO as he was called meaning, "The Bear" because of his huge frame, ran the cartel with his older brother Jesus up until his brother was assassinated by Lana and her crew. EL OSO with the help from someone inside of The Family has identified the top members of The Family and ordered them to be executed. JuJu, EL OSO's personal bodyguard was now in route to the mansion with eleven other desperados who were infuriated about what happened to Pepe and Jesus and were under orders to kill everyone there.

When Lana and the crew arrived at the mansion, they were greeted by O.G., a childhood friend of X and Kush's. Dr. Kadeisha was there also to look over Kish's wound. Lana was surprised to hear the news from O.G. as he escorted her and her crew through the house that the other heads of The Family were there, and she felt ecstatic when he informed her that X was coming soon too. She hadn't seen X in over a year.

Like the other three heads of The Family, Lana had her own wing in the mansion for her and her crew. As they all reached the French doors that separated Lana's wing from the rest of the house, O.G. pulled out about a half ounce of green.

"Here you go QB," O.G. said but Isis snatched it from him as they went into their pad.

"Thanks, Big O.G.," Isis said followed by Kish, Dr. Kadeisha, and Stretch.

Lana couldn't help but wonder what was going on for all the heads to be here at one time and then X was coming also. She waited for everybody to go through the doors before she asked O.G., "O.G. what's going on tonight, has something happened?"

"I don't know Queen," O.G. said, "I'm just following orders."

Lana interrupted, "From Kush?"

"No, Icy Bezel," O.G. replied, "he also said that he talked to X and that he would be here soon."

With hearing again that X was coming, all of Lana's worries melted away. As she was about to turn to go into her pad O.G. said, "And tell your bodyguard, this fam!"

Lana turned around and seen Stretch standing off to the side waiting. Lana just smiled and closed the French doors behind her cutting off the rest of the world. She fell right into the arms of Stretch and stayed there. Stretch leaned down and placed a passionate kiss on Lana's soft lips as he held her in his huge arms. To Lana, the kiss set off millions of tiny explosions of ecstasy throughout her entire body. Stretch picked Lana up effortlessly and took her into her bedroom.

They passed Isis rolling a blunt in the small living room on their way to Lana's room. *Isis just grinned and mumbled under her breath, "It's about damn time."*

Lana's room was the largest of her crews since she was the head of her department. Her room and everything in it was purple and black for royalty since she was the "Queen Bee." Stretch's eyes seen nothing but the king-sized canopied bed where he gently placed her and she pulled him down on top of her. In between slow succulent kisses they removed each other's shirts. Lana moaned as Stretch kissed, nibbled, and licked her from her neck to her breast, down to her belly button, then he slowly removed her pants and thong.

Immediately Stretch planted his face in between her legs, causing her to arch her back and shut her legs tight around his head like a vice. Lana was mesmerized and the overwhelming sensational feelings paralyzed her. Stretch continued kissing her thighs, down to her legs and onto her toes. Lana giggled with delightful pleasure as Stretch explored every inch of the softest body he had ever felt.

As he kissed and licked his way back up her body reaching her neck, then lips, Lana whispered, "Give it to me!"

Stretch gently caressed his rock-hard shaft back and forth between her clit and pussy causing Lana to thrash and buck. Feeling her wetness, Stretch's shaft got harder and throbbed now to reach its heaven. Sliding his dick slowly into Lana's hot, tight, and juicy pussy Stretch yelled out,

"Damn!" As he stroked slowly. Lana held on tight digging her nails into his back. On Stretch's 4th pump, Lana's phone rang.

"X gon' give it to you, gon' give it to you! X gon' give it to you…"

Lana forcefully pushed Stretch off of her to retrieve her phone that was on the floor in her pants. As she answered the phone Stretch saw her sweat juices run down her leg as he watched her stupidly from the bed.

"X!" Lana yelled out, "How you doing cuz? Where are you? Me and Ice have been worried about you! Are you here now at the mansion?"

X couldn't get one word in with Lana flooding him with comments and questions. Finally, X raised his voice over Lana's ranting, "Lanie! I miss you too cuz! You know everything always copesthetic," X continues while smiling, glad to speak with his only relative, "how's everything going with you and your crew?" Lana was so happy to hear from X that tears were streaming down her face.

Stretch staring at Lana's flawless body from behind, couldn't resist touching her soft flesh. He grabbed her butt softly. Lana smacked his hand and gave him a look with her eyes that killed any of his dreams for exploring and conquering her body tonight.

"We're all good cuz, Kish took a hit in the shoulder today, but she's alright."

X's smile quickly vanished, "Took a hit in the shoulder? From who?"

Nonchalantly Lana said, "It's handled cuz, we took care of it. Those Dominicans…"

X interrupted, "Hold up, you took care of who? Some Dominicans? Today?"

Lana puzzled, only said, "Yes."

X let out a loud sigh, "Please don't tell me his name was Jesus, Lanie!"

Lana stood motionless and speechless but her mind was moving a hundred miles an hour trying to figure out how X knew Jesus and what she had gotten herself into.

"Yes, that was his name," Lana said quietly, knowing something wasn't right. In seconds of racking her brain for a cause of her mishap, one name came to mind…Icey Bezzel!

X spat, "I knew something like this was goin to happen!"

Lana blurted out, "What? What's wrong cuz?"

"Get your team and O.G. and get the Fuck outta there Lanie," X said, "call me when you're on the road!"

Lana knew not to question X's orders even though she wanted some explanations. She knew answers would come in time. Eventually, X's moves always made sense. While Lana listened to X, she moved her naked body swiftly across the room stopping at a large painting on the wall of three African women painted by Carrie Mae Weems. She tapped the bottom of the frame and stepped to the side, the painted swung up revealing a cubbyhole in the wall with a depth of about a two feet. Inside were four shelves holding 9-millimeter pistols, clips, hollow points, and a stack of money. Stretch still gawked at Lana's beautiful body and complexion and didn't snap out of his trance until she grabbed one of her Flamma Bags by Salvatore Ferragamo and slid everything that was on the shelves into it.

"Those Dominicans WILL retaliate Lana! They're probably on their way NOW. Make moves and get ghost!" X said sternly. "Family Love!" X said before hanging up.

Lana replied, "Love our family."

Stretch waited patiently for Lana to end her phone call from X, he anticipated trouble from just hearing Lana's side of the conversation and got dressed immediately. After Lana grabbed everything from the hidden compartment and ended her call, Stretch watched and waited but Lana just stood there with her back to him as still as a statue. Stretch couldn't take the suspense of waiting and not knowing what was said or what was the next move.

"Lana. Lana? Lana!" Stretch yelled her name but Lana never budged. It looked like Lana was staring at the cell phone in her hand, but as Stretch got closer to the mannequin posed Lana, he realized she was looking at the hand from which her finger was severed. Stretch had seen Lana like this on a couple of occasions, in a coma like state but wide awake. Stretch felt sympathy and compassion for this beautiful girl which he loved so much, but that sympathy and compassion that he felt for her melted away in seconds and turned into hate and rage for the people who made her like this. Stretch grabbed Lana's shoulder and shook her causing her to jump like he had frightened her. Within seconds Lana regained her composure. Spinning around to face Stretch Lana reached into her bag and pulled out one 9-millimeters, cocked it, then passed the bag to Stretch.

"Pass these out to the crew and have them ready to go in one minute." Lana's facial expression and voice were emotionless as a robot as she stared directly into Stretch's eyes while spitting out directions like an army general.

Stretch transformed just as fast, from a lover to a soldier and absorbed the orders like a private and moved out to follow his commands. A minute later Lana emerged from her bedroom with a pistol in hand. Stretch, Isis, Kish and Dr. Kadeisha were already on their feet, armed with 9-millimeters and ready to go.

"I have lifesaving information," Lana said, "that the Dominicans will retaliate tonight, we have to move out ASAP."

Isis attempted to question, "Why…"

But Lana cut her off swiftly by saying, "There's a lot of unanswered questions that I'll get to the bottom of soon enough. My first priority is to keep us safe." With her head on a swivel looking into the eyes of each of them Lana continued, "Isis, come with me. Stretch, Doc, and Kish get a ride and meet us in five minutes back by the kennels. We have to get O.G…."

An ear-splitting thunderous clap drowned out all sound, shook the room and made the lightning flicker. "THEY'RE HERE!" Isis screamed.

WHERE'S X?

Detective Andrew Andis woke up in a cold sweat from a nightmarish sleep by his cell phone going off, playing taps notifying a new text message. Propping himself up against his headboard, the detective looked over at his alarm clock that shared the same nightstand with his cell phone, a pack of Camels, and a fifth of Tanqueray.

The clock read 4 a.m. "Shit!" The detective groaned as he reached past the cell phone and cigarettes and grabbed the half empty bottle of liquor. He unscrewed the top and took a whale of a shot. After frowning and grimacing as the potent liquor slid down his throat, he returned the cap, wiped a stream of liquor from the side his mouth, then picked up his phone.

For the first time in months, a smile spread across Detective Andie's face as he read the text message from Anthony Cruz, aka Big Sexy.

"I Know exactly where X is staying at, come ASAP!!!"

There were about 10 other messages from Big Sexy just like this one starting from two hours ago. The detective didn't like texting so he called Big Sexy, on the 5th ring he picked up.

Big Sexy sounded wide awake, "Hello Andie, I've been trying to reach y'all all night!"

Detective Andies didn't have time for small talk, he cut Big Sexy off, "Yea, yea I know, where is he?"

Big Sexy stuttered when he replied, "I…I…I'll have to show you, it's deep in the sticks. I've seen X with my own eyes, he's there! Let's get this Muthafucker!"

Up until about a year ago, Detective Andies just wanted to apprehend X, lock 'em up and throw away the key, but now he wanted to kill Yusef Watson better known as "X." He felt X was the cause of all his problems, personal, and professional ones. Detective Andies dreamt of retiring a hero with X collard or killed and then spending his last years on a tropical island.

Detective Andies thought of all this before he replied, "We'll be there in 20 min, be ready!" Then ended the call.

Immediately the detective lit a cigarette and called his young partner, Detective Way, but got no answer. Jumping out of bed he slipped on the same wrinkled clothes he wore yesterday that was scattered around on his bedroom floor. He kept trying to call his partner as he left his house on his way to Big Sexy. Detective Andies felt giddy and had butterfly's as he sped across the state to his informant. He pounded his steering wheel as he listened to Pantera's "Mouth of War."

When he got to the little bungalow, the sun was rising over the horizon and his emotions were amped up for the work he was about to put in. Detective Andies popped his trunk and rummaged through vigorously to find his bulletproof vest. After the vest was put on properly, the detective lit another cigarette, then punched in his partner's number on his phone. As he strolled to the front door of the house, unaware that this would be the last minutes of his life, Detective Andies turned the door knob and walked in.

Upon his third step into the house reality for him came to a snails' crawl. Precious seconds felt like minutes as the detective spotted Big Sexy sitting in a recliner eyes wide open with a single bullet hole in the center of his head and his dark empty mouth agape revealing no tongue. Dropping his phone from his ear and instinctively drawing his 45, Detective Andies saw himself from a far away and above place moving in slow motion. He saw a dark figure pop up from behind the same recliner Big Sexy was sitting in but it felt like his pistol weighed a ton.

As the detective swung his 45 up so it was parallel to the floor, he squeezed the trigger. Simultaneously with him firing off booming shots, the detective saw three flashes but heard nothing indicating that his opponent, the dark figure, had a silencer. The detective felt burning in his chest and his breathing was clipped.

After seeing the dark figure in the corner drop, Detective Andies felt weak instantly from the shots that he took. He tried to retrace his steps, backing out of the house. Just as the detective's foot touched the step, his backpedal came to a halt by a man sticking a pistol to his temple. The man took the detective's 45 and pushed him back into the house. Once back into the house, the man aggressively spun Detective Andies around, meeting the furious, penetrating eyes of X, his arch nemesis. The detective knew without a shadow of a doubt, that his life was over. Images of achievements, failures, and family from as far back as he could remember until the present, passed before Detective Andies' eyes within tenths of a second before he witnessed the brightest flash of light he had ever seen in his life.

VIOLATION

A dark trail of smoke followed the RPG projectile as it races towards the towering armed gates surrounding the mansion. Even before the smoke cleared and the debris landed three black Yukon's sped through the remains of the twisted and mangled gate. Fire blazed as the Yukon's passed the burnt-out shell of the guard shack. When the mansion was in sight the lead Yukon driver veered off the long driveway into the grass and stopped. The second and third Yukon followed the first into the grass but didn't stop, they continued in a wide circle. A quarter of the way around the mansion the second Yukon stopped, then the third one rode another quarter of the way around and then stopped too. The seven men in each SUV got out expeditiously and fanned out around the perimeter of the house. JuJu launched another RPG rocket, this time at the front of the mansion blasting a gigantic hole. As soon as the grenade found its mark, two more blasts were heard as if it was the cue for the two other

Dominicans that carried RPG's in different areas around the house to fire. Including JuJu, there were 21 cartel members, all armed with semi-automatic rifles, AR 15's, Sig Sauer S16's, Beretta ARX 160's, and Winchester 5KP pump action shotties. The Dominicans closed in on the house slowly walking making sure to eliminate anything or anyone inside the circumference.

Automatic gunfire rang out! Lana lead as Isis followed closely behind through the mansion. Occasionally passing "Family Members," male and female, running to hide or to get away but few willing to fight. Both women were crouched with each step they took, weapons up, eyes wide and ears strained. After they heard the three initial blast that seemed to signify the start of this ambush, Lana listened carefully at the estate's guard dogs barking which was huge massif. Lana visualized the dogs attacking the intruders, but seconds later she heard spritz of gunfire silencing the dogs. As gunfire echoed throughout the mansion, Lana and Isis moved against a wave of family members running from the action.

Lana tried to ask, "Have you seen O.G.?"

Just ahead at the end of the wide corridor that led to one of the three lounges in the mansion, shots sounded like they were being volleyed back and forth. Before reaching the lounge, Lana and Isis checked Icey Bezzel's office and saw two dead bodies. One was Sizzle and the other was a stringy hair Dominican with a beard.

When Lana and Isis arrived at where the corridor met with the lounge they stopped and squatted down before they peeked into the heavily flourished room, Lana saw four Dominicans. Two of them dragging a woman down an adjacent hall, Lana recognized her as an acquaintance of

Sizzle. The dark-skinned woman screamed, kicked and clawed but was no match for the two muscular men one of which paused for a second to backhand blood from the attractive woman's mouth. Then one of the Dominican's savagely ripped her white blouse off exposing her perfectly round breast. Lana continued to watch as one man drug the lady by her stretched arms while the other Dominican laughed wickedly following close behind careful to avoid the woman's kicks until the three of them faded down the hallway out of Lana's view.

More shots being fired from the other end of the lounge broke the trance Lana was in from witnessing a horror about to happen. Switching her attention to the other two Dominicans in the lounge, one using a sofa and the other a grand piano as cover while they continuously traded shots with someone behind the marble bar. Marble and glass shards rained down on the sole shooter behind the bar as a black fatigued clad Dominican sprayed the bars stock of colorful expensive bottles and all the mirrors that engulfed the wall.

Isis and Lana exchanged looks at one another briefly but spoke a whole conversation with their eye contact that was understood by both women. Lana eased out into the large room staying low making sure not to alert the Dominicans to her left that had a Family Member pinned down behind the bar. She followed the screams of the woman being raped down the hall.

Isis, now alone, still squatting put her pistol down to dig into the pockets of her black cargo pants and retrieved a blunt. She had stubbed the blunt out when Stretch had burst into the room telling her they had to go, with her blunt lit and burning evenly Isis took a slow and sure pull, picked up her 9-millimeter stood, then casually strolled out into the lounge. With the Dominican's attention focused on killing the lone shooter firing shots at them from behind the bar, they never felt the dangerous presence right behind them. Isis leveled her pistol high about to squeeze off a head shot into the Dominican that was closest to her, crouched down behind a piano. Isis took another pull from the blunt and immediately felt herself about to choke. Trying but failing to suppress an outburst, she coughed causing both Dominicans to turn in her direction. With her arm still extended Isis was able to squeeze off one shot to the nearest Dominican crumbling him to the floor. His body fell in an awkward position Isis thought, with his face firmly on the floor while his butt was in the air.

The other Dominican was bald headed and clean shaven, he cursed Isis calling her "Micons Puta" before swinging his big gun around with hatred in his eyes. Isis knew he had the advantage on her with the assault rifle before she could aim her pistol at the new target three shots were heard. Instantly Isis was aware that the shots fired were single shots from a pistol. The Dominican staggered a couple of steps toward Isis, then fell like a tree.

With the big man down, O.G. was revealed to Isis as he stood up from behind the bar with a smoking gun and a smile on his face.

"I just saved your Ass!" O.G. said while hopping over the bar.

"No!" Isis snapped back sharply, turning her back to him to hide her smile and how thrilled she actually was to see O.G.

"You would have been murked fo sho if I hadn't come!" O.G. yelled with a Kool-Aid smile then continued, "hold up, let me hit the 'L'!"

Lana didn't have to walk far down the corridor before witnessing the abomination. First hearing and then stepping slowly, Lana's first observation was seeing the two Dominican's assault rifles propped up against the wall like innocent pieces of furniture.

"Ontele, ontele cobron!" Lana heard as she kept moving forward, coming upon one Dominican standing with his back to Lana looking down in front of him with his manhood in his hand. He was watching his partner violate the terrified woman and waiting impatiently for his own turn to mount her. Empathy mixed with fury and blinding rage consumed Lana up completely, causing her first to see red then black.

ASIAN PERSUASION

Detective Claudius Way's tie hung loosely from his sweat-drenched shirt. His Hugo Boss suit was wrinkled and felt like a wet mop against his clammy skin. He threw his cards in, then ran his hand through his wet hair, and yelled, "Fuck!" It was 2 am, almost an hour since he first started ignoring calls from Big Sexy.

"BAD BOYS, BAD BOYS WHAT YOU GONNA DO? WHAT YOU GONNA..." Detective Way's phone chorused again the cops anthem as it rang. Frustrated with his lousy luck at the blackjack table he pressed power turning his phone off. Detective Claudius Way was held up in a gambling spot he frequented on the regular. The illegal gambling house was in a huge Victorian style house located in a sleepy town called Bucktown, owned by an Italian mobster, Joey "The Slugger" Gianni.

From Thursday to Sunday the house opened from 10 pm to 7 am. Joey, nickname "The Slugger" because he baseball batted another Italian boss to deaf in a restaurant over drug turf in the early 80s. The Slugger, now in his early 60s and in retirement, opened a house just to keep some cash rolling in and from totally tapping out his savings. Money came in steadily and with the local cops paid off the operation went smoothly without any major issues.

"Where's Joey?" Detective Way asked the dealer, a middle aged attractive red head.

After popping her chewing gum, a couple times, she informed the degenerate gambler with her New Jersey accent that, "Joey's in the office, probably getting a head job."

Detective Way knew exactly where Joey's office was because he had been in there numerous times for the same reason he is going now, a loan. Weaving his way through the various gambling tables of Blackjack, Craps, and Poker, Detective Way seen excited happy people he figured as winners. He also noticed people that were sad that looked like he felt, he quickly labeled them as the losers. Approaching a guarded staircase that led up to Joey's office, the detective was stopped and frisked by a humongous Italian that favored Luca Bronsa from the movie The Godfather.

The Luca Bronsa look-alike confiscated Detective Way's Glock 40.

"You'll get it back when you come back down," the big man said after receiving a look of frustration from the detective.

After the Luca Bronsa look-alike spoke quietly into the intercom on the wall, he let the detective up.

Once Detective Way reached the top of the stairs, another Italian stood not nearly as big as the first guard, but just as wide with the same massive girth, wearing an expensive suit, escorted him down a hall to a closed door. The stout, wide fellow banged on the door four times with his open hand. Thirty seconds later, surprisingly a gorgeous Asian woman opened the door wearing a black and pink colored kimono. She bowed, turned, and walked gracefully into the sparsely furnished room.

There was only two pieces of furniture in the room, an unoccupied brown leather couch and a massage table with The Slugger propped up talking on a cell phone naked with only a towel covering his bottom.

Detective Way was mesmerized by the beauty of the petite woman. As his eyes followed her into the room, her tan caramel complexed legs that the short kimono exposed left the detective deaf, dumb and mute. Dumbstruck, his hypnotized eyes move slowly down to her open toe stilettos as she moved around the massage table. Positioning herself so that she faced him, she began to knuckle The Slugger's back who was laid out between her and the detective. Oblivious to The Slugger ending his phone call and staring at him, the detective continued his gaze, now into the elfish face sporting Prada glasses that obscured her eyes from him.

"What can I do for you, CLAUDIUS?" The Slugger said holding his hands up to his mouth pretending to have a megaphone to his mouth to get the detective's attention.

Hearing The Slugger's nasal voice, what he had come to despise made Detective Way painstakingly remove his eyes from her and direct his attention to The Slugger.

It took the detective about 20 seconds before he could remember what he was doing there in the presence of the Italian.

"Oh! Nice to see you again Joey," the detective said embarrassed that he had been caught slippin.

The Slugger waved his hand like he was slashing through the Bullshit,

"You need a marker, right?"

Detective Way didn't say anything, his eyes shot up to the most beautiful woman he'd ever seen. "No," he finally said flatly.

"No?" The Slugger asked, "then what the Fuck do you want?"

HOT PURSUIT

"Are you alright?" Lana heard and felt Isis' comforting words as she placed her hand on Lana's shoulder.

Isis yelled, "Speed this Muthafucker up Stretch!"

Lana had an excruciating headache and her vision went from total darkness to being foggy. What Lana didn't know is that they were in one of the Dominicans Yukon's in a high-speed chase, fleeing from those same Dominicans that invaded The Family's mansion. The Dominicans had just rammed the back of their Yukon causing Lana to hit her head violently up against the back of the front seat. Disoriented and unable to focus her vision, Lana listened to the chaos going on around her which consisted of people cursing and yelling, guns being fired, and a dog barking. Lana tried to concentrate on where she was and how she got there but couldn't remember anything prior to her head hurting and Isis asking her was she alright. Lana's vision became blurry and fuzzy, then finally it started to clear up. Looking around bewildered, she quickly realized that they were in a truck with Stretch driving Kish was in the passenger's seat she herself was sandwiched between O.G. To her left, and Isis to her right. In the rear seat, she saw Dr. Kadeisha and a dark-skinned woman that she didn't recognize but that met her gaze, intensely staring directly into Lana's eyes.

"Here they come again," Dr. Kadeisha yelled out, "hold on y'all!"

There was a loud boom and everyone's head was thrown forward. The

Dominicans had rammed the back of their Yukon causing it to lurch forward and swerve. Stretch fought to gain control of the large SUV, steering aggressively right then left. Lana realized that the barking she heard was coming from a small mastiff cowering at her feet. Isis finished loading her 9mm from the bullets that were in Lana's Flamma Bag that sat open on her lap. She noticed Lana had gained her composure and had snapped out of what was now a normal occurrence of her slipping in and out of a blood-thirsty second personality. Isis slid the clip halfway into the 9mm and then banged it in completely with the palm of her left hand.

She winked at Lana and said, "Welcome back!"

Just before she reached up and pulled her torso out of the window, placing her butt where the glass disappears into the door. Isis fired repeatedly at the Dominicans in pursuit. O.G. did the same as Isis but out of the window to Lana's left. They both yelled out incoherent war cries as they emptied their clips. As soon as Isis and O.G.'s bullets were depleted they jumped back into their seats. Immediately return fire from the Dominicans pelted the SUV.

Everyone ducked as glass shattered and dull thud sounds engulfed them.

"Oh, Shit! I'm hit!" Stretch said through clenched teeth gripping his neck as blood instantly painted his hand red and soaked his shirt.

Lana leaned forward in her seat and caress Stretch's head. "Hold on Baby! We gon' make it out of this," Lana said into his ear.

Stretch just shook his head focusing on the rural deserted back roads as he sped down them hoping for a miracle.

When Lana thought things couldn't get any worst, Isis said in a low voice seemingly to herself, *"We're out of ammo."*

The Dominicans in the trailing Yukon acted as if they smelled the hopelessness of their prey. With their relentless will to kill and an unending supply of ammo the pursued greedily. The Dominicans tried desperately to pull to the side of Stretch, but he wouldn't allow them to flank him. Stretch stayed in the middle of the road and countered each maneuver the Dominicans tried to make. The pursuers went from side to side continuously bumping their bumper and steadily firing a stream of lead into the SUV. It was while everyone was on the floor of the Yukon taking cover from those shots, that Dr. Kadeisha made a discovery.

CHAPTER 9

By the time Detective Way reached his department issued Caprice, daybreak had broken. The brightness of the day and even the chirping of the birds irritated his alcohol infused senses. Drained physically and mentally from the long night, he knew without a shadow of a doubt that today would be one of his sick call days. The detective sat heavily in the car, he turned the ignition and smiled to himself as he saw the digits on the back of his hand. While pulling away from The Sluggers, he retrieved his cell phone from his pocket with the intentions of saving the lovely masseuse, Angie Wu's, number. The Detective had to Bullshit and bide his time with The Slugger until he had gotten his opportunity to talk to Angie Wu alone.

He got his moment about three hours ago when the stout Italian in the expensive suit entered the room briskly and spoke to The Slugger in a low tone.

"What! He did?" The Slugger said sounding shocked. He hopped up from the massage table and the towel covering him fell to the floor revealing red speedos. Stepping into his slacks he told Angie Wu, "This session will have to continue some other time Hun." The Slugger looked back toward the stout fellow, "Pay the lady!"

Immediately the man pulled out a mitten of cash and peeled off a couple hundred for the masseuse who bowed in return.

"Claudius!" The Slugger yelled slipping into his Gucci loafers with his shirt in hand, "you stay we have unfinished business."

The detective helped the masseuse pack up and carry her table to her car, which was an old Mustang. She blushed when he told her how beautiful she was, but only spoke a little, and with broken English. Detective Way practically begged to take her out to dinner.

Angie Wu shyly accepted, then took his hand in hers and jotted down her number, leaving him with two words and an innocent smile. "Call me."

Detective Way would have left from The Sluggers at that moment, if the Luca Brasi look alike didn't follow them out and stand waiting for him to finish with Angie Wu.

When he returned inside the house, The Slugger had relocated to a booth on the first floor with a fifth of Jack Daniels in front of him and two shot glasses.

"I've got your favorite!" The Slugger said pouring them both a shot, "the party has just begun."

Detective Way forced a smile, not liking what he was seeing because he knew The Slugger had something in mind. Not one for small talk, The Slugger spoke direct, "You still owe me Detective...for a hit."

Detective Way knew exactly what The Slugger was talking about but tried to tell him that the intended target wasn't hit, his friend was killed. There was no way the Detective could convince The Slugger that the assassination was botched because to The Slugger a body was a body. The nice, courteous, and thoughtful slugger, who minutes ago had just treated his friend with his favorite drink disappeared, and the real cunning, aggressive, and deadly one reared its head.

"I want the payment we agreed on!" The Slugger said while banging on the table in rhythm with every word of his demand.

Detective Way wasn't a fool. He knew cop or not, The Slugger and his goons had no problem killing him.

"You'll get your payment Joey," Detective Way continued as he poured himself another shot, "a shipment of guns, right?"

The Slugger's demeanor softened, "Roger that! All Pistols!"

As soon as his phone was turned on, the Detective didn't have a chance to save his newly acquired number. A steady stream of messages popped up and his ringtone kept repeating itself due to more messages from his partner. He immediately tried calling Andies to no avail, then called Big Sexy and got the same results. The detective sobered up fast with a feeling deep down in his gut, telling him that something was dreadfully wrong. Switching on the emergency strobe lights, he gunned the cruiser to Big Sexy's. He thought about calling in for back up but hesitated with the radio in his hand. Way knew that some of his underhanded tactics would be exposed if he got the whole of the department involved, but he also feared for his partners' life. Eventually, the Detective's conscience won the battle and he radioed in the location and possible officer in distress. He knew that the call would have policemen swarming around the house well before he got there. The Detective had come to grips that this decision could cost him his badge.

Twenty minutes later Detective Way pulled as close as he could to the small bungalow, which was about a two-minute walk from his car. The outside scene to him screamed homicide with all the uniformed officers milling around and the paramedics moving without a sense of urgency, but Detective Way wouldn't accept what his intuition told him. He flashed his badge and pushed through some uninformed rookies that didn't recognize him. The detective felt as if he was floating under the yellow tape and to the wide-open front door. His callousness, which he'd gained as a hardened detective, melted away at seeing the rearranged and disfigured face of his one-time mentor with a portion of his head blown off. Detective Way emptied all of the contents in his stomach right there on the spot.

HOT PURSUIT 2

Sissssssssss....smoke clouded inside the SUV from the discharge of the RPG as the hissing projectile covered the short distance between the two vehicles in the blink of an eye. O.G. had climbed all the way into the rear of the Yukon kicked out the bullet-riddled window aimed and fired the RPG at the Dominicans bearing down on them. Dr. Kadeisha discovered the RPG along with one grenade while ducking from the onslaught of automatic gunfire from the Dominican's.

Tapping O.G. on his back, who at the time was practically laying on the floor scared for his life, Dr. Kadeisha asked, "Will this help?"

When everyone saw what she was holding, hope was restored. Isis and O.G. bickered like kids as he climbed over the seat about who should take the shot. Lana's face was creased with worry and concern for Stretch, who by a dead man's standard looked bad, and was getting worse with every passing minute. Stretch was losing lots of blood. With both hands gripping the steering wheel, determination etched all over his face as he concentrated on getting his crew to safety.

At seeing O.G. position himself with the RPG on his shoulder, the Dominican driving the pursuing Yukon slammed on breaks screeching almost to a halt.

"SUCK THIS!" O.G. yelled as he fired the rocket off.

Everyone was in a hunched position cowering behind seats and heard what sounded like two trains colliding when the projectile hit the Yukon in the grill and exploded. With a delayed reaction of about ten seconds, after the shrill cry of mangled steel, a choir of cheers arouses from everybody.

Stretch had dug deep and had given his all to stay alive until Lana was safe. When all the cheers sounded off indicating the demise of their foes, Stretch let go and stopped the fight for his life, giving in to the calm and peacefulness he felt pulling at him.

Just as the cheers went up, Lana caressing Stretch's head said to him, "Pull over Babe, so Doc can look at you."

Stretch looked at Lana, his eyes seemed to be apologizing and she watched his chest heave as he took his last breath. The shock had taken her ability to speak or call out to anyone. Lana just reacted by reaching over the seat and going for the steering wheel. Kish in the passenger's seat was turned around talking to Isis when she saw Lana lunge over the seat. A split second after Lana made her move, Kish dove for the wheel also but neither women were fast enough to alter and right their course. A sharp curve was coming up just as Stretch's life expired. The big SUV soared through the air crashing and flipping three times into the edge of the forest.

ICY BEZEL

What was left of Icy Bezel's suit was in tatters. He tore what remained of his Gucci shirt and threw it to the ground as he dashed through the woods. Only a sweat-drenched wife beater clung to his muscular physic while he gasped for air running and stumbling through thick brush and vines in the dense forest. Icy stopped after he had ran for a good five minutes to listen for if anybody was coming after him. He heard nothing but the sound of crickets chirping in the pitch-black darkness. Icy cursed himself at being so I and underestimating the sharpness of Kush and X. His ambition must have shone brightly. *He thought, "Damn, just when I was so close to being ALL the way out of this Shit!"* Seeing that no one was trailing him, Icy tucked his chrome 45 and continued on walking gingerly through the forest not caring what direction he was headed in as long as it wasn't back to the mansion. Luckily, Icy Bezel never stopped carrying a pistol, as he grew up from a young thug on Nat Turner Drive to a boss who was now known up and down the east coast. If he hadn't had his pistol, Icy knew he would have been dead now just like his friend Sizzle. He bit down on his lip as he thought about the rapid change of fortune that had just swept over him.

When the Dominicans bombarded the mansion, he, Sizzle, Ms. Rae (Sizzle's lover), and their accountant had just minutes' prior transferred all of The Families funds from the various business fronts The Family owned into an offshore account in the Cayman Islands.

While toasting to their future the first blast rocked the mansion, causing the lights to flicker and then go out permanently. Before any of them knew what was going on a wild-haired man kicked in the office door unleashing a hailstorm of bullets. Sizzle got laced up with holes as he jumped in front of Ms. Rae to protect her from getting shot. Like it was second nature, Icy took cover while drawing his 45, cocked, aimed, and shot. The single shot he let off was a head shot that blasted the Dominicans brains onto the wall and all over Ms. Rae. She cried out shrilly and ran hysterically out of the room. Blood gargled and spilled out of Sizzles mouth as he tried desperately and in vain to grasp on to his fading life.

Icy Bezel shook his head in disbelief as his partner managed to get out the words out, "Get…get…our money," before his life was extinguished.

Icy went after Ms. Rae, cautiously checking rooms and moving quietly down the dark corridors. Gunfire, screams, and cries echoed through the mansion. Hearing screams and someone talking in Spanish coming in his direction, Icy looked around for a quick hiding place. Icy eased the door open to a small linen closet and squeezed himself in. There wasn't enough room for the door to close so he just pulled it as close as he could get it and held it. Peeping through the crack in the door, Icy saw Ms. Rae being dragged by one Dominican as his friend laughed wickedly following close behind. Icy figured he could take both of them, especially since they would have their pants down soon from the looks of it.

Just as he was about to slide out of the closet Icy saw someone moving slowly past real quietly. Straining his eyes, he recognized the Queen B, Lana, slinking past going into the direction of the Dominican's and Ms. Rae. Tired of walking Icy pulled his pistol out and sat down on the ground, propping himself up against a tree. A chill ran through his body causing him to shutter all over as he saw a flashback of what Lana, the Queen B, did to that Dominican. Icy Bezel had eased out of the closet after Lana crept passed, just in time to witness the sick act she was committing. Before he could make his presence known and get Ms. Rae out, he heard more voices coming down the hall. He quickly and quietly returned to the linen closet seconds before he saw O.G. and that other crazy Bitch Isis go passed.

"I know why you tryna act so mean Girl, you don't got to fight it," Icy heard O.G. saying.

"Boi please!" was all Isis said.

Then O.G. shouted, "What the Fuck!" Icy knew they had come upon Lana, the Dominican's, and Ms. Rae.

As Icy dozed off to sleep there in the dark forest all he could think about was how he was gonna get Ms. Rae back so he could get all that money. He, Sizzle and Ms. Rae each had a different passcode, and to get the account open each code has to be revealed. Icy knew that without a shadow of a doubt that Ms. Rae smart Ass knew Sizzle's code. Just like he knew that he didn't have a chance in hell of getting Ms. Rae from those crazy Bitches tonight without getting himself killed. Icy stayed hid until they were gone, then following their same exit route, and found safe passage out of the mansion. Head in his chest, Icy drifted into a restless sleep filled with obstacles, pain, and rewards. His long-time friends' X and Kush fueled his hate and the millions at his fingertips drove him blindly, unconsciously, as it would soon do the same when he awoke.

DINNER FOR TWO

Claudius Way didn't bat an eye when Chief Lynch fired him, taking away his badge and police issued firearm. Claudius felt as if all that he had learned at the department was training for what was to come. He dove headlong into the underworld like it was his birthright. Claudius, with a replica badge and his personal Glock, didn't miss a beat. He ran down on and kicked in every drug dealer's door he knew as if he hadn't been relieved from his job. Only instead of locking them up, he acted as if he was doing the dealer a favor by just confiscating the drugs and money. In a matter of weeks, Claudius Way went from a young cocky cop earning a meager wage to a self-proclaimed "Super Gangster." He already accumulated 3 kilos of coke, 1 kilo of heroin, 4 pounds of weed, and over $30,000 in dirty drug money that made him feel invincible.

The very same day he got canned Claudius did the exact opposite of what his old self would have done, called Angie Wu. They went out to dinner that night at a place called Jimmy's Grill. A place for ordinary people that want good food in a casual setting. Claudius did most of the talking. Angie Wu spoke very little, besides questions and answers that only consisted of a couple words at a time. Claudius spilled his guts to Angie practically telling his life story. He summed his journey up to that very date with her, with revenge in his heart for his partner and defiance in his bones. He could tell that Angie liked him even though she didn't express it in words.

The former detective made her smile and blush and by the time their first date was over she was talking and opening up a lot more.

"My father owned a prosperous antique business called the Jade Dragon. It was in Seaford, right off the Nanticoke River. His name was Kazutaka Bonzi, the most brilliant and virtuous person I've ever known, he's still an inspiration to me."

As Claudius and Angie Wu laid in his bed bodies tangled and twisted together, he stared at the ceiling remembering what she had told him about her father. His conscious was eating him up, even more, now that they had become intimate, "Angie!"

"Yes," she answered, without lifting her head from his chest. Claudius took his hand and placed it under her chin and gently tilted her head up so he could see her eyes. "I have a confession to make to you," Claudius said, as Angie Wu sat up giving him her full attention.

"What is it?"

Claudius took a deep breath, "I was covering that case...of your father being murdered...and I found out who killed him...but, turned a blind eye...for a favor." Claudius felt awful and ashamed, he braced himself for an eruption of emotions and rejection from Angie. But to his astonishment, a smile spread across her lips and he face lit up.

"I know you were covering my father's case, and I had already had my assumptions of why The Slugger wasn't arrested."

With Angie Wu mentioning The Sluggers name Claudius' facial expression showed his surprise that she knew who was behind her father's death.

"I'm so glad you've admitted that to me. I know you are a different person than what you were back then," Angie continued speaking looking into Claudius' eyes, "I also know that he killed my father because my father refused to pay The Sluggers so-called property/protection tax. My father always told me everything." Angie Wu's voice suddenly dropped and the sweet innocent face became rigid as she spoke with conviction. "An arrest is not the justice I have in mind for Joey The Slugger."

For the second time that night they had mind-blowing, out of this world sex. Fate had brought them together, but revenge sealed their bond making them feel as if they were one. His objectives were now hers and hers his.

OPERATION RESCUE

Everyone was alive, from the looks of it with non-life-threatening injuries from the accident. Lana figured she'd lost consciousness for a short period of time. She awoke to the puppy mastiff licking her face. Lana couldn't move her left leg and it was in excruciating pain. She assumed it was broken. Isis' face was painted crimson with blood. She had a huge gash across her cheek, it was wide open. O.G. only had minor cuts and scrapes, while Dr. Kadeisha and Ms. Rae seemed to not have a scratch on them. Kish had gotten thrown completely out of the SUV. She was up moving around, driven most likely by pure adrenaline with the back of her head split open. O.G. found his phone a few yards from where the SUV stopped flipping. He immediately called Kush, telling him what happened, what road they were on, and to hurry and pick them up before someone or the police rode pass. Lana cried as her and Isis held one another, not because of the pain from her leg injury but for Stretch's death. At this point, she realized she truly was in love with him because Lana had never felt the pain she was feeling now.

Twenty minutes later, two black Yukon's rounded the curb and came to an abrupt stop. As the day was breaking, Lana and the crew were huddled together looking weary and helpless. *All of them had the same thought, "We're dead!"* In the lead Yukon, a Spanish looking woman hopped out looking worried.

Lana's first thought was, "She looks Dominican. Who is she?" But her thoughts were answered out loud by Isis.

"Evita!" Isis said with disgust, "why is she here?"

X shot out of the second Yukon, running straight to Lana and Isis. Lana hadn't seen her cousin in almost 2 years. They hugged briefly and she told him her leg was broken. He picked her up and put her in the middle seat in one of the SUVs. Lana protested about leaving Stretches body behind until X and O.G. put his body in the back of the Yukon.

"O.G.," X said, "Lana, Evita, and Ms. Rae are riding with me."

"I'm riding with y'all too!" Isis said holding her face with tears in her eyes.

X gave her a sharp and hateful look and said, "Not now Ice, we'll talk back at the spot!"

Evita sighed feign, being impatient with X speaking to Isis.

Dr. Kadeisha yelled as everyone was getting into the SUV's, "We have to go to my house X, almost everyone needs medical attention and they can't wait much longer!"

X stopped as he was about to shut his door to the Yukon and thought for a second, then replied, "Alright let's go!"

X sped down the back roads and through small towns as traffic became more and more common the brighter the sun shone. Dr. Kadeisha's home was located on the outskirts of the town of Bridgeville.

"Lanie!" X called out, looking at her and the dog on her lap through the rear-view mirror. Lana sat with her leg stretched out in the second seat and Ms. Rae was in the back of her. Lana had a feeling X was about to say something that she wouldn't like, she saw his eyes dart from her to Ms. Rae in the rear-view mirror. "Things have changed Lanie, we have new allies," X said sounding like he was selling the idea, "we will rebuild, bigger and stronger than ever!" As he spoke Lana noticed the girl Isis called Evita reach over and grab X's hand.

"What the Fuck is going on cuz?" Lana spat, not being able to hold back any longer.

"Who's she? And what are you talking about!" Lana said, now yelling.

"That's what I'm tryna tell you!" X said yelling as well, "Icy Bezel and Sizzle turned on us…"

Before he finished his sentence, Ms. Rae blurted out, "That's not true! You and Kush betrayed the whole family!"

Evita turned in her seat and was now yelling as weIat Ms. Rae, "Shut up...Shut up! Before I smack the taste out ya mouth!"

Lana didn't know Ms. Rae personally but she could tell she was all books and smarts and no fight.

Although she still was in major pain from her broken leg and her grief from Stretch's death was overbearing, she still spoke as if nothing bothered her except that someone was threatening a dear friend.

"You will not smack her!" Lana said, "just who do you think you are?"

"She's with the enemy!" Evita said pointing at Ms. Rae.

"No!" Lana shouted back, "she's with me!"

"Everyone calm down," X said looking around at all three women. "Lanie, Icy, and Sizzle with the help of her," X said pointing back at Ms. Rae with his thumb, "have wiped out each and every account we had! She's gonna give me my money one way or another!" X said staring directly at Ms. Rae in the rear-view.

"Sizzle's dead!" Ms. Rae said, "You killed him!" She screamed busting out into tears.

Lana looked into X's eyes in the rear-view and seen a look of regret. His eyes dropped when Ms. Rae made the accusation.

"You sent those animals to our mansion, they killed Stretch! You killed Stretch!" Lana said, her voice dying out before she finished her sentence.

She was putting the pieces together to the puzzle, thinking, "That's why you called...you didn't care if I got out of there or not...you were just clearing your conscious, convincing yourself that you gave me, your flesh and blood, a chance."

"No! No! Lana, it wasn't like that. I didn't mean for any of you to get hurt," X said pulling into Dr. Kadeisha's driveway.

A flood of thoughts and emotions erupted and overflowed within Lana. She cried, cursed, yelled and screamed, "I'm done with you! I'm out, X! Stretch I'm so sorry I love you!" Lana was still balling when Dr. Kadeisha and Isis came to their SUV.

"What happened?" Isis said immediately, hugging Lana.

"Nothin!" X said getting out of the SUV.

"Come on Lana, we got you," Dr. Kadeisha said as her, Isis, and Ms. Rae helped her into her home and down to the basement.

In her basement, Dr. Kadeisha had a state-of-the-art medical facility, courtesy of The Family. She had performed countless surgeries and removed thousands of bullets for The Family in her years of being affiliated with them.

Down in the basement, while Dr. Kadeisha cleaned out Isis' and Kish's wounds, Lana pulled Ms. Rae close to her and said, "Don't leave my side if you want to live."

X was on his cell phone at the bottom of the steps that had brought them down to the basement. Evita was by his side with her hands on her hips. Lana saw X looked towards her a couple of times while he spoke in hush tones that she couldn't hear but knew just about what the conversation was about.

"Alright everyone upstairs!" Dr. Kadeisha said while looking at O.G., X, and Evita, "I can't work with you all standing around."

X looked up from his phone call about to protest but he seemed to say to himself as he peered around the spotless basement, "The only way out is the stairs up to the house."

He reluctantly nodded to Evita and O.G. "You!" he said pointing at Ms. Rae, "come with me."

Dr. Kadeisha said hastily, "I need her. She gonna help me with the cast for Lana."

X walked up the stairs slowly but not before giving one more demand, "Doc, I need this to happen like yesterday. We have to get a move on it!"

Dr. Kadeisha replied, "I won't be long X."

Evita followed him up and O.G. trailed. O.G. winked his eye at the ladies, then blew a kiss to Isis.

As soon as Lana heard the door shut upstairs, she turned to Dr. Kadeisha, "You have to get us outta here Doc!"

Dr. Kadeisha gave her a reassuring look, "I told you I got you, Baby. Why do you think I sent them away?"

CHAPTER 10

"What the Fuck is it Pauly? I thought you were capable of running Shit for a freakin hour or two while I got my back fixed!" The Slugger yelled at the stout wide Italian in the Armani suit. He propped himself up on his elbows as he spoke to Pauly from Angie Wu's massage table.

"Sorry Boss."

The burly no neck man The Slugger called Pauly said, "It's Detective Way, he says he's got a payment for you and he wants to give it to you personally. He also lost a couple grand downstairs on the tables."

Angie Wu continued massaging The Sluggers back. The Slugger had nothing but underwear on and a towel covering his bottom half. Angie Wu's hair hung down naturally touching her slender shoulders that were adorned by a black and gold Kimono. All The Slugger heard when Pauly was speaking was that "Detective Way had a payment."

"Send him up," The Slugger said, then spoke over his shoulder to Angie Wu, "this interruption won't be long Sweetie." Angie Wu just bowed her head with a smile while keeping her hands moving up and down his back.

Two minutes later, Claudius came through the door followed by Pauly carrying a duffel bag. Claudius Way looked like he had been on a 2 or 3-day binge in his expensive but wrinkled suit, stubble face, unkept hair and he reeked of alcohol.

"The prodigal son returns with gifts!" The Slugger said, with a lizard-like smile on his face.

Pauly walked with the bag over to where The Slugger was at on the massage table and held it open under The Slugger's face. After The

Slugger peered into the bag full of handguns for a couple seconds, he shook his head showing his approval. Pauly closed the bag and exited the room with it, shutting the door behind him, leaving The Slugger, Claudius, and Angie Wu.

Claudius sat on the same brown leather couch he had in his last visit there. Claudius gave off the air of a man that had had way too much to drink. The Slugger watched him like an owl observing his rodent prey but wore that same lizard-like smile.

"Please don't tell me," The Slugger said, "that you brought gifts but you need a favor?"

Claudius shook his head exaggeratedly and hiccupped. The Slugger laughed like he had been told a joke that no one else in the room had heard. Angie Wu didn't stop her magical hands as The Slugger laughed and talked on, "since it took you such a long time to get square with me, I need 2 dollars on every dollar I give you!"

Claudius' eyes bulged. "Two dollars on every dollar, C'mon on man! That's steep…but I'll take it."

The Slugger still grinning responded by saying, "I knew you would!" Then laughed.

Claudius hiccupped again, "With customers like me…I know you have to be a millionaire."

"My dear degenerate gambling Detective, you are so right," The Slugger said laughing uncontrollably now.

"Well, I need all of that!" Claudius said.

"Say What? I didn't hear you, Detective," The Slugger said still laughing loud.

"I said we need all of that!" Claudius said a little louder and clearer, so he could hear him over his own laughter.

With that The Slugger heard two mechanically distinctive clicks behind him, then he felt cold hard metal press up against the back of his skull. The Sluggers laughter, then his smile evaporated. Claudius stood and just put one finger over his lips, "Shhh."

Claudius was looking in The Sluggers direction but his eyes were glued to the magnificent creature Angie Wu. She had her Kimono wide open displaying her black lace lingerie that Claudius had bought her. Along her rib cages, were two holsters on each side, that's how she smuggled in their silence 9-millimeters.

"Damn you Sexy Woman!" Claudius said to Angie Wu, who blushed at his compliment.

Angie Wu moved from the side of The Slugger so she could join Claudius who stood in the front of the massage table facing The Slugger. She and Claudius kissed as she handed him one of the pistols. All the while, she never dropped her left arm that held her 9millimeter that was aimed at The Slugger.

The Slugger looked pale, baffled, and sick. "Isn't she sexiest thing you ever laid eyes on?" Claudius asked The Slugger whose mouth was wide open.

The Slugger just stared speechlessly. Angie Wu reached back with both hands wrapped around the pistol grip and swung the 9millimeter like it was a Louisville slugger and connected with The Sluggers' face. The blow split The Sluggers forehead from his hairline to his eyelash.

"Answer the man you, Pig; don't you hear him speakin to you?" Angie

Wu spat venomously.

The Slugger shook his head up and down repeatedly as he held on to the massage table for dear life, looking like a deer stuck in headlights. Claudius smacked Angie Wu's Ass and she moved back to the position she was in when she was massaging The Slugger, only now she jammed the pistol into his side. Claudius backed up to the wall till his left arm was flush with the door frame.

"Call that Big Ape," Angie Wu said into the ear of The Slugger.

The Slugger's head was leaking and he was in a state of shock about what was happening to him. Angie Wu jammed the silenced barrel deeper and harder into his side.

The Slugger yelped, then obliged, "Pauly!"

Three seconds later the man built like an offensive tackle for the Philadelphia Eagles came through the door. He took about 8 steps into the room stopping a foot in front of The Slugger. It took precisely 2 seconds before the big man registered The Slugger's split face and then Pauly heard the door shut behind him. Spinning around, Pauly saw Claudius standing in front of the closed door with a pistol pointed at him. Without a word Pauly charged at Claudius like a raging bull. PFFF… PFFF…PFFF…PFFF! Claudius let his pistol do the talking. All four shots entered Pauly's massive chest and gut but none slowed him down. Pauly's face look like a demon had possessed him. He closed the distance in three giant steps, then wrapped a huge and powerful hand around Claudius' neck and with his other hand Pauly hammered on Claudius' face. Claudius' pistol flew from his hand as Big Pauly's blows wreaked havoc on him. Pauly looked like he was holding a rag doll. Just as suddenly as

Pauly's assault began, his arms dropped to his side and then the big man crumbled falling on top of Claudius. As Claudius slid from underneath the dead weight of Pauly, he saw a perfect hole in the center in the back of Pauly's head.

"Thanks, Baby," Claudius said to Angie Wu as he rubbed his throat, checked his face with his hand to make sure he wasn't bleeding, then he picked up his pistol.

Pauly's actions seemed to restore some confidence in The Slugger. Staring at the shaken-up Claudius, he said, "Detective, you two won't make it outta here alive, you're fools to try to rob me!"

Claudius walked over to The Slugger and stared down at him as Angie Wu snatched the untied belt out of her kimono loops and stuffed it in The Sluggers' mouth.

"First of all, I am not a detective anymore," Claudius said to the physically agitated Slugger who was trying desperately to act calm. Claudius kept talking, "and second of all...we don't want your money!"

Angie Wu acted as if that was her cue. She moved from aside The Slugger and joined Claudius. They both faced the now trembling old man with a gag in his mouth sitting up on a massage table with only a white towel draped over his lap.

"Do you remember Kazutaka? Angie Wu asked.

"Kazutaka Bonzi?" At hearing the name Bonzi, The Slugger's eyes told that he indeed remembered him.

"Yes!" Angie Wu continued, "I know you would!" PFFF...PFFF!

"UGGH...UGGH!" The Slugger screams were muffled by the gag. Angie Wu had shot him in both of his shoulders.

Shut up! Shut up!" Angie Wu hissed.

The Slugger looked to Claudius; his eyes pleaded him for help. Claudius only shrugged his shoulders.

"My father was a good man!" Angie Wu said as she began to walk back and forth in front of The Slugger. Without warning, she raised her weapon again. PFFFF!

"UGGH...UGH!" Angie Wu shot The Slugger in his right thigh. She then walked over to The Slugger who was now almost doubled over sobbing in agony. He was bleeding like a stuck pig from the three gunshot wounds and from his split head. The Slugger pleaded for his life behind the gag, his hands weren't tied but he dared not remove it from his mouth.

Angie Wu pulled the gag outta his mouth and stuck her pistol to his head. "Any last words Pig?" she asked.

The Slugger could barely speak through the pain; his breathing was labored, "Claudius...I...I have a million cash...take it and let me live..."

"Sorry!" Claudius said, "I thought I made myself clear, we don't want your money. We want your life!"

"HOLD! HOLD ON!" The Slugger yelled looking at Angie Wu who held her pistol to his head. "In my pocket is the key to my yacht...The Claira Lee, she's docked in the Seaford Marina and...on her is a million cash...spare me…please!"

PFFF…Angie Wu blew his brains onto the wall. The Sluggers body followed his head off of the table down to the floor. Angie Wu went directly to the coat rack where The Sluggers clothes were draped on. Digging into the pockets, she fished out a key ring with three keys on it. Angie Wu dangled the yacht keys into the air, "To sail off into the sunset with, together."

"First, we got to get up outta here," Claudius said as he folded down her massage table. They walked out of The Sluggers gambling house together as they had done before. With Claudius helping her by carrying her massage table. The only difference than before is, as they made small talk and descended out of the house their fingers stayed on the triggers of their concealed pistols.

THE GREAT ESCAPE

X paced back and forth in Dr. Kadeisha's living room like a caged lion. Evita sat on the doc's plush tan sofa reading a Hip Hop Weekly, and O.G. was busy in the kitchen fixing himself a roast beef sandwich. X's thoughts were on the millions that he and The Family had made together that were now so close to being all his and Kush's. He could taste the freedom and opportunities those millions represented. X had made up his mind, he didn't want to kill, rob, or be a part of the drug and criminal underworld anymore. Those numbers that that Bitch Ms. Rae had in her head were X's key to a new and long life. Just as he had decided that he was about to go down into the basement to check on the doctor's progress, his phone rang.

Downstairs in the basement, with Isis' face and Kish's head, stitched up, they both helped Dr. Kadeisha wrap an air cast around Lana's entire leg.

"This break is too severe for me to do anything to except stabilize it. We don't have enough time to fix it," Dr. Kadeisha said with her brow creased and beads of sweat racing down her far head to her face. While pumping air into the cast Dr. Kadeisha explained to Kish, Isis, and Ms.

Rae what to do. "Y'all gonna have to get Lana to a hospital as fast as possible!"

Lana sat up from her laid-back position on the bed. "You're going with us Doc. You have to!" Lana said, grimacing from the overbearing pain.

Dr. Kadeisha shook her head, "No Baby. I'm tired of running around, getting shot at, and almost being killed. I'll just slow you guys up anyway."

Dr. Kadeisha saw the sadness and fear in Lana's eyes, as she quipped. "I'll be alright Lana, as soon as this is all over, we'll vacation together," the doctor said with a pretty but forced smile. After that, the doctor left and went to a cabinet and came back with two pills. "Take this for the pain," Dr. Kadeisha said, "they'll kick in a few, right after you're out of here."

With that being said, the doctor told Isis and Kish to help Lana up and for Ms. Rae to follow her. Lana hopped painfully on her one good leg, as Isis and Kish took the brunt of her weight, positioning themselves under each of her arms helping Lana move quickly behind Dr. Kadeisha and Ms. Rae.

"I had a feeling this would come in handy," Dr. Kadeisha said as she stopped in front of a set of wooden bunk beds. "I got this built years ago after I started doing work for The Family."

"What, these beds?" Ms. Rae asked looking puzzled and confused.

Dr. Kadeisha ignored her and pointed to the ceiling above the bunks. "Get up there on that top bunk and turn that latch, then push with all your might."

Ms. Rae didn't see any latch until she climbed onto the top bunk, then looked at the ceiling more closely and carefully. The walls and ceiling to the basement were all whitewashed as well as the latch. Ms. Rae couldn't believe her eyes when she spotted the latch, but she was amazed even more when she turned on it. With a little elbow grease and some grunting, she pushed the trap door open.

"Come on y'all, the garage is up here!" Ms. Rae said excitedly.

Kish and Isis struggled trying to help Lana get up the ladder to the top bunk.

"Take my minivan," Dr. Kadeisha said as the girls finally got Lana to the top bunk, "the keys are in there."

"I love you Doc!" Lana said as she was pushed by Isis and Kish through the door to Ms. Rae who was pulling her up in the garage. Dr. Kadeisha let out a sigh of relief as Isis and then Kish vanished through the portal.

X ended his phone call with Kush and went directly to the mini bar Dr. Kadeisha had in her living room. He didn't even take the time to pour himself a shot, he grabbed the first gallon he laid eyes on, which was E&J. With both hands, X tilted the gallon and guzzled. Evita, looking up from her seated position, knew X had been under immense pressure as of lately and even more now that he was in the process of tearing down his old life and rebuilding a new one.

"X, what's up Baby?" Evita cooed as she was behind her man and rubbing his back in no time.

X sat the liquor down, wiped his mouth with the back of his hand and then retrieved his pistol from his waistline.

"Go home Evita," X said without emotion and with a blank look on his face. Evita was just about to attempt to protest as she took a half step forward. X said, "Porvavor!" Pleadingly.

Evita rested her head on X's back, then wrapped her arms around him caressing his chest with her hands. Seconds later, without another word she was walking out the door. Minutes prior, when X was chugging down the E&J, his mind sought out and searched until he had satisfied his conscience with a justifiable reason for killing his own flesh and blood, Lana. The millions, retiring from crime, growing old, married with kids and grandkids! Thoughts that until recently had never crossed his mind.

With enough reason to account for a lifetime of his sku oggeryery, X, without giving O.G. a heads up stormed to the basements door. Moving like a juggernaut, he didn't break stride as he kicked the basement door off its hinges. Taking the steps, three at a time, down until he reached the basement, X immediately came to a halt. Dr. Kadeisha was the only person in the basement, she sat on one of the three medical beds with her feet dangling looking like she didn't have a care in the world.

"Where are they?" X screamed, his eyes darting left to right scanning every inch of the basement.

Evita yelled from the top of the basement stairs, "The tires are flat in both trucks X!"

X's questions, demands, and words became incoherent with each step he took towards the doctor. By the time X was inches away from Dr. Kadeisha's face he was in full rampage mode.

Dr. Kadeisha just looked up into the furious eyes of X unafraid and said, "Let the poor girls go Yusef..."

Before she could finish her statement, X reached out and grabbed a hold of her neck. Dr. Kadeisha never took her eyes off of X's eyes and didn't put up a struggle or plead for mercy.

As X squeezed and squeezed, he ranted on and on. "Where the Fuck are they? Imma kill all of you! Tell me!"

O.G. rushed down into the basement and with some effort pride X's hands from the doctor's throat but just as soon as X's left hand released its vice like grip, he raised his pistol welding right hand. Before O.G. had an idea or inkling of X's intentions a shot was fired off. The momentum of the bullet upon impact to the doctor's forehead knocked her back so it looked as though she was just laid-back relaxing on the bed.

O.G. shoved X causing him to stumble. "What the Fuck you do that for X?" O.G. asked, looking at the doctor's body with sympathy written all over his face as he shook his head. X's reaction was in voluntary as he righted himself from O.G.'s push and came up with his pistol aimed at his friend. O.G. said nothing but his facial expression spoke loud and clear. It showed hurt, disappointment, regret, and most importantly a look like his awareness had been boosted up by volumes. X dropped his arm, pushed passed O.G., and darted up the stairs. Once outside, X saw that all the tires were indeed flattened on both SUV's and as he looked across the flat land noticed a dot, miles away that no doubt was Lana and the girls. Enraged, X emptied his whole clip into the clouds as he screamed in frustration.

SURVEILLANCE

Slouched down in an old 1985 Buick Century, Claudius Way sipped from a crown royal bottle and stared out of his rain streaked windshield into the stormy night life inside the projects known as the gardens. Angie Wu sat Indian style in the passenger seat, both behind the cars dark tints.

They've been on a stakeout for the last two weeks, waiting for Sista Vic to lead them to X. Claudius could tell Angie Wu was getting restless, and tired of being cooped up with nothing happening, as he was alert and watching their surrounding not taking his eyes off Sista Vic's apartment.

Angie Wu's eyes were glued to a porno on her phone. Claudius, out the corner of his eye, saw Angie Wu stroke the crotch of her leopard print Kardashian Collection tights and purr like a kitten. He fought with all his might to resist her allure and to not put her in the backseat for a real live porno. Claudius looked over to Angie Wu, she felt his eyes on her within seconds and returned his gaze. They both smiled as they read one another's mind, then he turned the radio up to drown out the sound of the porno.

Claudius' mind drifted back to the last couple of months, which both of them have agreed were the best of their lives. After they had murdered The Slugger, Claudius surprised Angie Wu with a vacation to Disney World. As long as Angie Wu was happy, Claudius was ecstatic. He lived to make and see her smile. He proposed to her while they were on a roller coaster. Claudius didn't plan on asking her to marry him. The thought had never crossed his mind, until the second before he blurted out the question. He thought that he had done something wrong because Angie Wu burst out into tears. She didn't say, "Yes," until after the ride stopped and she had gained her composure. She embarrassed him afterwards by telling everybody they came in contact with that Claudius had asked her to marry him and she said yes. Claudius couldn't believe that he had found the perfect woman and it blew his mind that soon they would be married. Not counting the money Claudius had accumulated in the last 5 months, they could start and build a new life with the million in The Claira Lee, The Sluggers yacht. That's exactly what they planned on doing after this one last loose end is clipped.

Claudius sat up pressing his face to the windshield so fast he spilled Crown Royal on his red Lacoste shirt and startled Angie Wu. He had just spotted Sista Vic coming out of her apartment with an umbrella and a small duffel bag heading towards her silver infinity.

"Showtime!" Claudius said as he eased his car into drive.

He took a nice shot from the Crown Royal bottle, then pulled out after Sista Vic, but not before letting three cars go in between his Buick Century and her infinity. Angie Wu lit up a joint, put down her phone, and then turned the radio off. She hoped that after being on a stakeout for two weeks and following Sista Vic around all over God's green earth, that she would finally lead them to X.

Angie Wu had heard many vicious and murderous stories of X from Claudius. She hated and despised X even more than Claudius. Twenty minutes into the ride, Claudius had to fall back and put even more distance in between them and Sista Vic because they had trailed her onto the rural MD back roads with very little traffic. They were about a full minute behind Sista Vic, they could see her break lights when she slowed for curves. Suddenly and without warning, Claudius hit his right signal light and turned into a driveway.

"What are you doin'? We'll lose her!" Angie Wu protested.

Claudius immediately killed the Buick's lights, slammed the car into park and turned his body almost completely around in the seat. Angie Wu turned in her seat also, so she could see what he was looking for. About 3 seconds after she had turned in her seat, she saw a car go past. The car didn't have its headlights on. Angie Wu knew she had looked behind them as they followed Sista Vic out of habit, but never noticed another car on their trail. Claudius backed the Buick out of the driveway and swung it in the direction that Sista Vic and the mystery car went in, only now he didn't cut on his headlights. Claudius was hunched over the steering wheel straining his eyes against the rain and the darkness. He still could see the brake lights of the mystery car and Sista Vic's infinity when they slowed down or took curves.

After a half hour of riding in the darkness and in silence, Claudius and Angie Wu saw Sista Vic turn off the road. The mystery car slowed almost to a crawl. Claudius came to a complete stop, as did the mystery car that was trailing Sista Vic. Claudius and Angie Wu assumed that the mystery man or woman was getting an eye full, making sure X was at the house. Just as soon as the mystery car's break lights went off, the car disappeared fast from Claudius' and Angie Wu's sight. Claudius crept the Buick past the residence, which was a 2-story brick house, and recognized X, who was giving Sista Vic a hug.

"We're gonna do this bastard ASAP before we are beaten to the punch by whoever was in that car!" Claudius told Angie Wu as they rode on.

SURPRISE 2

Evita came skipping down the stairs; her Lucenda 16-inch boots clicked with every step she took. Coming into the dining room, she spotted X at the large oak table. She stood across the room from him with her hands on her hips and her feet wide apart in a Superman pose. X didn't lift his head up from the pile of money on the table that he was counting.

Evita sashayed over to the table and around to where X was seated, making sure the heels to her boots clicked loud and clear on the hardwood floors.

"Who was at the door?" Evita asked, already knowing the answer.

Not looking up X answered, "It was Sista Vic, she bought me the protection money from them clowns on Bacon Street!"

Evita, not getting the results she wanted, which was to get X to look at her, just made her try harder.

"Do you like my new boots?" she asked.

"Yes," X replied still counting, "Damn, I thought I had a money counter here!"

X was snatching bills from one hand to the other when Evita stuck a boot on the table in front of him. X's eyes followed the tall black boot up to a bare cinnamon colored leg and further up to the naked body of Evita. A body and face that would have the goddess Aphrodite jealous. The money fell from X's hands as a Kool Aid smile spread across his lips.

"Come here Momma!" X said while scooting his chair back so Evita could move between him and the table.

Evita's hands instantly went for X's button-down Sean John shirt. As she stood over the seated X, she pulled the shirt over his head leaving him only in a body fitting wife beater. X just sat back admiring his Dominican's queen perfect body. Evita squatted down between X's legs and unbuckled his belt, unbuttoned the pants, then pulled out his manhood. She spat on his erect tower and watched as her saliva slowly dribbled down it.

"You nasty!" X said with a smile.

Looking up into her man's eyes, Evita kissed X's flesh, then engulfed it into her mouth. She moaned as her head moved slowly, up and down. X could only stand a couple minutes of this delightful sensation. He was anxious to be inside Evita's sweetness. Grabbing a fist full of Evita's wavy hair, X pulled her head back and then kissed her hungrily. As X stood up, still with a grip on Evita's beautiful hair, she arose also. Once Evita was standing, X pushed her back into the table, she complied and sat her soft exceptional Ass on the oak table. X pulled up her right leg, letting her heeled boot rest on the tabletop as he dropped to his knees. X gently stroked Evita's pearl button with his tongue while caressing her wet and hot universe with his fingers. X continued until he felt Evita tremble and her sweet nectar gushed out of her forming a small puddle on the oak table and staining up some of the 20's and 50's he was counting. X stood up straight and pulled Evita towards him forcefully, plunging his rock wood right into her wet softness. They both let out loud sounds of pure pleasure as soon as he entered her, and she received him. X moved sure and true, starting slow and easy, then moving in a circular motion with his hips, then finishing his thrust with force. X repeated this motion as he held both of her legs up. Evita's small pretty face rested on his shoulder. X laid Evita back firmly on the table cushioned by the dead presidents sprawled all over it. Evita spread both of her butt cheeks apart while X slid in and out.

"Si poppa!"

Their exclusive climatic soiree landed them upstairs an hour later in their king size bed, exhausted. Evita's sweaty and silky feeling body was stretched out on top of X's and her head rested on his chest listening to his heartbeat. Sitting up, Evita straddled X, the same position she was in minutes prior coaxing X in Spanish. She reached over to her nightstand retrieving a blunt and a lighter. Evita had rolled the blunt an hour earlier, while she went over in her mind what she would do and say to X to get her way. As she was lighting the blunt, X watched amused. Evita took a couple of pulls and looked at the cherry on the blunt to make sure it was burning evenly, then passed it to X. X took the marijuana from Evita. She watched him from her position above inhale and exhale the intoxicating plant, and X looking up at her watched her too as he puffed heavily.

"What?" they both said in unison.

X burst out laughing, "What?"

Evita said, "What's funny?"

"Because I know you like a book," X said passing Evita the blunt.

"What's that supposed to mean?" Evita said taking a tiny pull from the blunt.

"You seduced me when we were young playing a teacher with no panties and bra because you wanted me to get you a Mickey Mouse!"

Evita giggled saying, "That is not true."

X continued, "Then when you were in college and wanted that Benz you dressed up like Wonder Woman!" Evita passed the blunt back to X as they both laughed thinking about old times.

"You know you loved me as Wonder Woman!" Evita said.

X coughed from the weed, nodding his head in agreement, "I copped the Benz didn't I?" Still coughing X asked, "so what's up now? What do you want Evita?"

With X asking that question, Evita's smile vanished and the cheerfulness in her eyes turned into sorrow.

"I want my family! Our family!" Evita said, now tears in her eyes. "I'm afraid for you Yusef. Jesus is dead. You know Roberto and I have never been close like Jesus and I was. Roberto's evil!"

X attempted to speak but Evita held up her hand, "Let me finish." X laid back against the headboard and continued to smoke while listening. Evita continued, "We don't need to be a part of this Bullshit anymore, we have money X! You have money! I have money! We, not the same two broke hungry kids wearing clothes too big and shoes too small!"

X's blank facial expression did not change the whole time Evita spoke, he just continued blowing smoke as she spilled her heart out. Evita had already assumed that her persuasive heart felt pleas wouldn't penetrate the calloused heart of X. Just like he knew her like a book, Evita knew X as well, probably more than he knew himself.

"I'm pregnant Yusef!"

FUTURE GENERATIONS

The suspension of the Range Rover sprang up when El Oso stepped out of the SUV. He walked down a small gravel driveway that led up to a tan double wide mobile home. Two of his best shooters accompanied him, the twins, Fame and Money. Both scanned their surroundings looking left to right for any threats to their boss. They saw no threats, only kids playing in yards further up the dead-end street and an old man cutting grass at the house next door. El Oso loathed coming to the country. He couldn't stand the smell of manure in the fields and all the trees; an assassin could be anywhere. Ever since he took full control over the Dominican Cartel, and his brother Jesus' murder, El Oso has been paranoid about leaving his safe confines of the blocks the Cartel owned in the City of Wilmington Delaware. A middle-aged brown skin woman, that looked to El Oso in her mid-40's, sat on the steps of the double wide with a beer in one hand and a joint in the other.

As soon as El Oso and the twins stepped out of the range she said, "He's in the back!" El Oso turned to the twins and made a hand gesture telling them to relax and sit tight. Both of them leaned against the truck unconcerned about anything not pertaining to El Oso and they wouldn't move until their next command.

Fame and Money weren't big men at all, they both stood at 5'5 and at first glance, a person would think they were harmless. They always wore designer clothes with loud and bright colors. They were identical, except Money never talked much, but Fame did enough Shit talking for the both of them, hence their names. Their eyes were the only indicators that they were stone cold killers, and one could find more solace in the eye of a crocodile. Wearing a plaid sports jacket, gray T-shirt, and charcoal color tuxedo pants, all by Tom Ford except for his Brooks Brothers loafers, El Oso felt out of place as soon as he stepped from the SUV and into all of the nature that surrounded him. He didn't expect to go around the side of the mobile home and see Kush in an apron standing over a Bar-B-Q grill but that's exactly what he saw. The two had become friends over the past couple of years unbeknownst to Jesus while he was alive and to X from Kush's Family.

El Oso and Kush first encountered one another through the dealings of X and Jesus. Then, they bumped into each other at the Powerhouse concert. After that, they had exchanged numbers and went out to a couple clubs and other engagements together, all the while, becoming more and more acquainted with one another until they ultimately felt comfortable enough to start doing business. Now, with the two of them sharing the same common goals, fears, and mutual investments, they were closer than brothers and more dangerous. The tantalizing aroma of the sweet-smelling meat on the grill hit El Oso in the face when he came into the backyard. El Oso smiled as he approached his friend Kush, who wore a stained-up apron over a wife beater, baggy Rocawear jeans, and scuffed up Timbs. El Oso reminded himself that this is how these country boys dress when they are in their environment. They greeted each other with a firm handshake.

Removing his Gucci shades El Oso said while looking down at the grill, "You country boys sure know how to eat good!"

Kush replied, "Paula Dean ain't got Shit on me!" Then he took a swig from the champagne bottle in his left hand as he turned the drumsticks over with a fork in his right. "Bring a couple of those paper plates from of that table so we can eat Oso."

Kush had called El Oso late the night before and told him that they needed to speak face to face as soon as possible but wouldn't tell El Oso anything else.

El Oso hoped that Kush had good news, like Lana the Queen Bee was dead and that Ms. Rae was in their custody. It had been almost two months since they had disappeared. Minutes later, El Oso and Kush were seated at a glass patio table in the same backyard eating BBQ chicken, hamburgers, and baked beans. They both washed their meals down with their own bottle of Moet, drinking straight out the bottle.

Kush broke the silence first, "I know where the girls are being held up at Oso."

"Where?" El Oso said licking BBQ sauce off his fingers.

"First," Kush said as he leaned back in his chair while pushing his empty plate to the side, then lighting a long fat blunt. "I don't think X can go through with the request you made in eliminating the Queen Bee," he paused taking a long pull and exhaled a thick cloud of smoke, "both of our families have made sacrifices to get to this point. But...I don't think X is willing to do what has to be done for us to reach the next phase in this game...which is having enough money for our great, great grandkids to live off of."

The two men moods became sober fast with the seriousness of the conversation. Their eyes locked and the lighthearted smiles evaporated. After a long moment of silence Kush continued, "X has to die...in order for us to kill Lana and get to Ms. Rae and that money!"

El Oso nodded grimly and held up his bottle for a toast, "To our future generations!"

CHAPTER 11

"Aaahhh Aaahh!" a chilling shrill pierced the quiet and serene summer day inside the small one storied house in Blades, DE. Ms. Rae hurried into the room where Lana had been taking a nap but now was thrashing violently from side to side in the queen size bed while kicking and swinging.

Ms. Rae grabbed Lana by the shoulders and shook her hard while calling her name out at the same time, "Lana! Lana! Wake up Lana!"

Lana's eyes popped open looking fierce, bewildered and at the same time frightened. Lana looked around at her surroundings and at the worried face staring back at her like it was her first time ever laying eyes on both.

"Who are you? And, where am I?" Lana demanded to know.

"Lana it's me, Rae! We in Blades Girl remember?" Ms. Rae said loud and clear staring into Lana's non comprehensive eyes that she could tell was searching frantically for answers. Ms. Rae kept speaking, seeing that Lana still was confused. This was the first time this had occurred while Ms. Rae was alone. This had happened three other times but Isis and Kish were here and Lana snapped back to her rational thinking fast. Ms. Rae understood that Lana was suffering from some serious post dramatic stress.

"Remember me? You saved my life, Lana. I was about to get raped..."

Lana interjected, finishing Ms. Rae's sentence, "And I sodomized one of those Pigs with his own rifle!"

Lana stared blankly into nowhere for about 20 more seconds in silence reliving that night, then she started blinking away the fogginess until she was her normal self. Ms. Rae saw the softness return to Lana's beautiful eyes and face. Looking around the room Lana said, "Sorry...sometimes...I'm not myself," with an embarrassed crooked smile. Ms. Rae wiped Lana's sweat beaded brow.

"Don't apologize to me or anyone else Lana! You don't owe anyone an apology. Matter a fact," Ms. Rae said as she helped Lana stand, "I never got a chance to thank you."

Lana waved Ms. Rae's thank you off as she hobbled out of the room with Ms. Rae right behind her.

"No Lana stop and look at me!" Ms. Rae yelled at Lana causing her to stop and look at her.

"What?" Lana said with a smirk on her face.

"Thank You! You didn't even know me, you coulda left me to die!"

"Well, now we do know each other...and as you just witnessed, I'm kinda Fucked up...I'm not a good person Rae!" Lana said as she turned and went into the bathroom leaving behind a speechless Ms. Rae.

Isis and Kish had left an hour earlier saying they were going to buy some weed to smoke. For the last two weeks, the two of them had been leaving behind Ms. Rae and Lana at the house almost every day. Ms. Rae didn't mind staying behind with Lana who now wore a cast on a left leg. Besides, Ms. Rae was still worried about X and she didn't think Kish and Isis liked her too much. After they all fled from X at Dr. Kadeisha's, they took Lana straight to the hospital. Lana's femur was broken in two and she had to receive an operation where a metal rod and pins were inserted into her leg. Isis, Kish, and Ms. Rae stayed in the waiting room during the operation and didn't leave Lana's side afterwards until the sedatives wore off and she opened her eyes. Then Lana told Isis to rent a crib close by so she could be close to the hospital. That was two months ago. Lana had gotten the pins removed only two days before and was happy to be moving around much easier. Lana and Ms. Rae had gotten to know one another more and more each day they spent together. One day, the month before, while Lana was immobile due to the contraption that circled her thigh which stabilized and protected the pins in her leg, her and Ms. Rae played a game of Tonk.

"You Cheated!" Lana yelled when Ms. Rae won a third straight game.

"I've never cheated a day in my life, Girl!" Ms. Rae said as she shuffled the cards.

"Whatever!" Lana said laughing, "you've cheated on a boyfriend?"

"No!"

"Well, I know you've cheated on a test before in school?"

Ms. Rae thought as she dealt the cards, then answered, "No, I don't think so."

"Damn it took you a minute to think about it," Lana said jokingly, "how long ago was it that you were in school?"

"Actually, I'm still in school Lana," Ms. Rae said as she put down a spread of three Queens, "I'll receive my Ph.D. in another year. But not if things continue like this." Ms. Rae noticed the smile disappeared off of Lana's face and she got quiet as she laid down a spread of three aces and dropped with the last ace and duce.

"What's the matter?" Ms. Rae asked, "you finally won and you look like I beat you again."

"Nothing," Lana said as she scooped all of the cards off the table to shuffle them.

After a couple minutes of silence and well into their next game Lana finally spoke again, "I went to college too."

"You did?" Ms. Rae asked totally surprised.

"But I didn't finish," Lana said, "I wanted to be a teacher."

"You look like you really enjoyed going," Ms. Rae said. Lana shook her head in agreement with a single smile spreading across her face.

"You should go back and get that degree, Girl!"

Lana thought about that conversation as she stared back at herself in the mirror, a matter of fact for the last month going back to college was all she thought about. When Lana limped out of the bathroom the mastiff that she had had named Milli, who all the other girls had to convince her that she saved back at the mansion, charged Lana happy to see her owner. Milli had ridden with Kish and Isis so Lana knew that they had come back with some weed that she most desperately wanted. Isis, Kish, and Ms. Rae were already at the table when Lana slowly came down the hall to join them.

"What's up Bitches," Lana said playfully to Kish and Isis while sitting down at the table.

"Wut up?" Kish replied but Isis didn't say a word, she just gave Lana a head nod.

Both women were rolling blunts. Lana had been feeling bad vibes from the two women for weeks now, but just put it off as them being upset about The Family crumbling. But at this instance when she walked into the dining room and sat down Lana felt the suffocating tension, and the ill contempt.

Isis and Kish giggled and smirked amongst themselves as Lana and

Ms. Rae looked at one another with questionable looks. Ignoring Isis and Kish's blatant disrespect, Lana took the deck of cards that were in the center of the table, shuffled them, and then dealt everyone in for a game of spades. Isis finished rolling her blunt, ran the lit lighter back and forth over the length of it, then lit it. After Isis took a long and hard pull off of the blunt, she exhaled, blowing a thick blue cloud of smoke from her nose and mouth. She stared at the cards Lana had dealt her that laid face down on the table in front of her.

Sucking her teeth, Isis looked at Lana who had her cards fanned out in her hand.

"I don't want to play cards," Isis said being openly insensitive.

Before Lana could object, Isis asked, "What are we gonna do Lana?" while she continued to slowly inhale and exhale the sweet-smelling cannabis.

"What do you mean?" a baffled Lana asked back.

Isis exchanged a quick look with Kish who at the time was lighting the blunt she had rolled. Even though their eye contact was subtle, Lana caught it and recognized immediately that whatever the two had been smoldering about in their time alone together was about to erupt like a volcano.

"Me and Kish trying to make moves Sis, we tired of sitting here doing nothing and hiding or whatever," Isis stated vehemently.

"I know you supposed to be healing up and grieving but we didn't sign on to protect her!" Isis said as she pointed at Ms. Rae with the smoking blunt.

Before Isis could catch her breath to throw another barrage of her self-proclaimed truths a wounded looking Lana spoke with her emotions being held in check by a thin vile.

"Sorry Ice if I'm holding y'all up...I thought...just thought that friends and family were for...tough times."

Lana saw the smug looks on both Kish and Isis' face and only one word popped into her mind. "Why?" In a matter of seconds, Lana came to the conclusion that this wasn't family she was dealing with but the enemy, and she would address them like such.

Standing up bracing herself on the table, she leaned over and snatched the blunt right out of Isis' mouth. With an evil eye, Lana asked, "What's up with y'all?"

Kish blurted out, "At least we can make money with X! I took a bullet on the last job and didn't get a dime yet, plus I never got shot Fucking with X."

"Rae!" Lana yelled without taking her eyes off of Isis, "get me my Flamma Bag please!"

Ms. Rae jumped up fast and walked quickly into Lana's room. She came back within a matter of seconds with the same bag Lana had stuffed with guns, bullets, and money back at The Families mansion. The bag was stained with Stretch's blood. Ms. Rae handed the bag to Lana but instead of sitting back in her seat, stood beside the seated Lana. Lana reached into the bag and pulled out a couple bundles of rubber banded knots of money.

"Here!" Lana tossed it to Kish, "that's fifteen G's!" Then she dug in the bag again and threw Isis a little larger knot.

"That's twenty, for the last job and for renting this crib and furnishing it! Y'all can take y'all Asses right back to X!" Lana yelled as she stood back up fast with some difficulty from her broken leg.

With that, Lana yelled, "Milli!" The mastiff laying on the floor quietly stood up alert on all fours and a throaty growl was heard.

"Get out!" Lana screamed. Kish and Isis slowly stood up, and moved cautiously toward the exit, not taking their eyes off of Milli.

When Isis reached the door she said, "You've changed! Everyone knows you crazy, but your gonna disown your own flesh and blood and your best friends for someone you don't even know!"

Lana yelled, "MILLI, GET 'EM!" The huge puppy shot through the house at full speed headed for Isis at the front door.

Isis hurriedly stepped out of the house and slammed the door closed just before the dog reached it. Lana and Ms. Rae sat in silence and listened to Isis and Kish's engine start. Once Lana heard tires squeal, leaving the yard she burst out into tears and bawled like a baby!

LOVE BIRDS

Claudius Way awoke at 3 a.m. from a restless five-hour sleep. He was anxious to eradicate X from this world.

"Just this one last loose end," Claudius told himself, "then I'll be sailing away into the sunset."

He looked over his shoulder as he sat on the edge of the bed, at the naked Angie Wu sound asleep intertwined within the blankets revealing a sexy smooth leg here and a slim delicate arm there. Claudius wished they could just get up right now and sail away on The Clara Lee, but his conscious wouldn't allow him to live happily ever after without killing X. He felt that he owed it to his late friend and mentor Andis and to society. Claudius went into the small bathroom to shower. They were at a sleazy motel in Federalsburg MD. twenty minutes away from the house were X was at. All Claudius could think about as the water from the shower hit his head and ran down his face and body was all the money he had seen while aboard the yacht The Clara Lee. Immediately after he and Angie Wu killed The Slugger, they drove out to the Seaford Marina in search of the yacht that supposedly held a million dollars. It didn't take them long to spot the 44-foot Cabin Cruiser. They boarded her, then went below into the cabin using one of the keys that they had lifted from The Slugger. Claudius and Angie Wu searched the yacht high and low for the money and for any signs of secret compartments. After over an hour of ransacking every nook and cranny of the yacht, they both laid exhausted on the carpeted floor below inside the cabin. Being familiar with yachts and boats Angie Wu thought of one last place that they hadn't checked on the Clara Lee where a million could be stashed away. Claudius had given up on the treasure hunt content with owning a new yacht. He busied himself by opening up a vintage bottle of wine from The Slugger's fifty or so aged bottles lying in a rack. Angie Wu went off still searching, not believing The Slugger had lied to them.

About 15 minutes later Angie Wu ran into the cabin out of breath startling Claudius who had almost emptied a bottle of The Sluggers finest.

"Bring your pistol, I think I've found something!" Angie Wu said breathing hard. Claudius followed her still holding the bottle of wine, along with his silenced 45 out to the rear of the yacht.

"Shoot that off Baby!" Angie Wu said pointing to a large lock.

"What's in there?" Claudius asked, taking a swig from the bottle.

"The engine," Angie responded. Claudius gave her a pained look like he was saying, "Why?"

Angie Wu answered his expression verbally, "No one locks up their engine!"

"PFFF PFFF!" the two shots dismantled the lock. Angie Wu eagerly with trembling hands removed the broken pieces and raised the big hatch.

"WOW!" they both said in unison.

Angie Wu was already awake when Claudius finished showering. She was just about to enter the bathroom shower as he was walking out wearing only a towel. Angie Wu stood on her tippy toes and kissed Claudius and he held her for a brief moment.

"The rest of our lives start when we get back on that boat today!" Claudius said quietly and without conviction. Angie Wu just smiled with the thought of her and him in paradise with no worries as she rested her head on his chest.

As Angie went into the bathroom, Claudius noticed that she had laid out on the bed black fatigues and her all black cat suit along with her silenced 9-millimeter Beretta 92F with his 45. Claudius Way let a huge grin spread across his lips.

"My Baby's the Shit. She ready!" he said to himself.

Half an hour later they were suited up in all black and strapped headed for X's with nothing but bad intentions in mind. Riding in silence under the light of the moon in the old Buick Century, Claudius went over in his mind what they were gonna do. They were just gonna stash the car away somewhere on the side of the road or field a mile or two from X's house, then huff it through the woods. Once they were situated in X's back yard concealed by the woods, they would watch and wait for their opportunity.

The little belongings they both cherished were already aboard The Clara Lee. A couple of sentimental valuables, which were mostly pictures of loved ones, all their money, a couple of outfits, and cosmetics made up everything they owned. Claudius Way and Angie Wu were rare. They were content with the unselfish love they shared for one another. Rich as they were now or penniless, they would be the same two love birds. It's ironic because, with all the money that they've accumulated together since they met, the most consistent thought on both of their minds was that they could give the other the world now.

CHANGE OF PLANS

Evita woke up early in the best mood in her life. X was still sound asleep so Evita decided to have her man wake up feeling incredible. She stuck her head under the covers about a minute later. X's eyes popped open with a smile on his face as he watched the blanket rise and fall below his waist. Today's the day that they would board a plane, fly out to Texas never to return again. X had taken a week to sell his properties and to get all his money and accounts in order. They were to meet with a Realtor in Texas on the following day. X was just as excited as Evita to finally be starting a new life with his very own family. He promised Evita that X, his alter ego, would be left in DE once they boarded their flight and from there on, Yusef, her husband, and family man, would take over. He even surprised Evita the night before with a 3-karat engagement ring as he got on one knee and proposed to her while they were out to dinner at a cozy restaurant in Seaford called the Dairy Bar. With X's mind being made up to leave his criminal ways behind and start a new life, he couldn't be on that plane soon enough. He had a feeling coming from deep down within him that he wouldn't leave DE alive. His intuition told him to get far away and as soon as possible as he could. X still had that feeling as he showered with his beautiful wife to be but hid it behind a smile while he silently prayed.

A moving company left two days ago headed for Texas with all of their clothes and possessions that they couldn't live without. The house was being sold completely furnished so they didn't have that headache of having to sell the furniture. At about 7:30 am, X was dressed with their matching gator suitcases loaded up in the only car that they hadn't sold between them, a cherry red CLA-ClASS Benz.

"Come on woman let's go!" X yelled up the stairs to Evita who sat in front of a vanity mirror doing her hair and makeup.

After she checked the time she yelled back downstairs, "It isn't even 8 o'clock yet, our plane doesn't leave until 12 Boi!"

X paced back and forth, anxious to leave the house and get as much space between his old life that held all of his transgressions and his new life that had started once Evita said she was pregnant.

"Hurry up! I have somewhere I want to take you!" X yelled back up trying to get Evita to come on, "It's a surprise!"

"Okay!" Evita said, "give me a few Babe!"

X sighed loudly shaking his head, he knew that meant about another hour if he was lucky. Not knowing what to do with himself, he started rolling a blunt with trembling hands. As soon as X took the first toke, O.G.'s facial expression appeared in his mind of when he drew his pistol on him at the Doc's. X felt guilty for not telling O.G. that he was about to disappear for good. Apparently, O.G. was his only real homeboy.

X had started to see Kush for who he truly was and what he held important over everything. Money! X came to this conclusion about Kush after he had time to think about his longtime friend ordering him to kill his own cousin and most loyal and capable henchman Lana the Queen Bee. X pulled out his iPhone and called O.G.

It rang about 5 times before X heard a sleepy voice say, "Wuts up Dog?"

"Wut up O.G.!" X said, immediately smiling at hearing his friend's voice.

"Why you call me so early man, you know I don't get up till 11 or 12!" O.G said with a yawn. There was a pause because X couldn't utter the simple words that were in his head and heart.

"Yo?" O.G. spat, thinking the line went dead.

"Yo," X answered, "I'm sorry...sorry for pointing that gat at you Dog!"

O.G. downplayed how he had felt about it. "Ain't nothing X, I know you my man and Shit was hectic..."

Before X could reassure his friend that his loyalty still resided with him 100 percent and that he was about to board a plane with plans to never return, he heard tires screech and a multiple of car doors close.

"What the Fuck!" X said as he peeped out his living room window.

X's heart dropped at the sight of Kush, El Oso, and two Spanish goons carrying Mac10's who he quickly identified as the murderous identical twins, Fame and Money. What frightened X the most was the manor and attitude in which the small entourage moved.

Claudius Way and Angie Wu watched X intently about 50 yards away hidden by the thick foliage as he loaded two suitcases into a red Benz.

Angie Wu was ready to pounce on X as soon as she saw him, she nudged Claudius hard in his side with her elbow indicating that she thought it was the perfect time to kill him. Angie Wu and Claudius knew that they wanted to get this done and over with. Like killing The Slugger was personal for her; this assassination was the same for him. Claudius felt he had to be up close and intimate so he could look into X's eyes as his life faded away. Claudius held up one finger telling Angie Wu to wait. Turning his head towards Angie Wu, Claudius looked into her beautiful black eyes as they were almost concealed to him due to the black and green camouflaged paint she wore.

Without speaking any words Angie Wu understood loud and clear just as if Claudius verbally shouted, "I got this Baby, just follow my lead and watch my back." Angie Wu nodded, telling Claudius she understood.

As soon as they saw X return back into the house, Angie Wu followed Claudius slowly and quietly along the inside of the forest line until they were facing the side of the house. Claudius Way and Angie Wu emerged quickly from their cover of the trees and didn't stop running until they sat crouched with their backs flat up against the side of X's house. After unholstering their weapons, they moved slow and sure, with knees bent, backs hunched, and pistols pointed to the ground. They stayed as close as possible to the house as they bent the corner and moved parallel to the back of the house, eyes fixed only on the French doors that X had walked through just minutes ago. Just as Claudius and Angie Wu reached and kneeled beside the deck that led up to the French doors the roar of car engines made them duck for cover. Tires screeching to a halt, then multiple doors opening and closing broke the early morning harmonious sounds of birds singing and a woodpecker hammering. Claudius and Angie couldn't see the people who had just arrived from beneath the deck, but Claudius translated fast the Spanish that he heard one man speak.

"Wait until I leave with my sister, then you kill him!"

"O.G. these Muthafuckers coming to kill me...Fucking Kush..." X yelled. His voice sounding shockingly frightful, even to himself as he threw the phone at one of his sofas.

"What? What you talking about?" O.G. now sitting up in his bed asked, but X was already gone. O.G. heard X call out for Evita as he continued to listen on the phone line and then he heard a familiar sound that he knew well.

"BOOM!" The twin, Fame, kicked in the French doors knocking both doors off their hinges. He led the pack as him and his brother, Money, moved expeditiously through the house until they found X. X was at the bottom of the stairs about to go up to Evita when both twins appeared with their sinister looking Mac10's pointing at him. X cursed himself for allowing someone to catch him slipping without his pistol. But just yesterday, Evita had made a big fuss about him always having to have a gun on him and said that he should get used to living a life where being armed wasn't necessary. Last night before he went to bed, X threw his pistol in the garbage dumpster. When he woke this morning he had had second thoughts and went outside to retrieve but the trash collectors had come early and the container was empty. Hence X's paranoia and anxiousness to leave the house so soon. He was unarmed for the first time since being a kid. Evita was on her way downstairs to see what the loud commotion was but stopped halfway down when she saw the love of her life being held at gun point.

"Yusef? What's goin' on..." Evita's words were lost in her thoughts at seeing her brother, El Oso Roberto, coming up the steps to her. Kush stepped into X's view from the dining room in the back of the stoic faced twins. X's eyes bore into Kush like a drill, but his focus quickly switched to El Oso and Evita. El Oso didn't say a word, he just picked Evita up easily and placed her over his shoulder like a sack of potatoes. Evita screamed for him to put her down and screamed for Yusef as she pounded on his back. X took half a step forward but was met with instant accountability. Money rammed the butt of the Mac10 into X's face causing X to drop to one knee. X felt powerless as he watched El Oso walk right past him taking the most important person in his life away, and there was nothing he could do about it.

Evita's and X's eyes locked for a brief second where the time for them stood still and a regret shared, "We're too late in getting out!"

Kush smiled as he looked back and forth from X's face to El Oso who carried the beautiful woman through the broken French doors as she cried and screamed out in Spanish and English.

"Sorry Bro," Kush said, "business is business and right now...you holding up my millions." Then he turned and headed for the French doors. Just before he walked out of the house, Kush turned back around to face X who stood with a twin on each side of him and said, "See you in Hell Bro!"

With Kush gone the twins backed off of X putting a good five feet between them and him. All three of them stood in silence, X's eyes not leaving the twins or their lethal macs.

He waited to feel the hot lead penetrate and pierce his flesh and vital organs. He would not beg for his life, actually, X welcomed the coming tranquility.

"What the Fuck y'all waiting for?" X yelled at the two dull looking twins. Their facial expressions read like they weren't doing much more than about to take a walk in the park.

Hearing a motor start outside, then the sound of a vehicle fading away until it was gone was when one of the twins finally spoke.

"K, Cobron, de head r de stomach?" Fame asked as X noticed both twins planted their feet bracing their stances for when they discharged the powerful weapons. X didn't take one step back, he left his head higher, closed his eyes and said a prayer.

SHOWTIME

Claudius and Angie Wu peeped through the wooden spindles of the deck from their kneeled position when they heard a woman screaming, pleading and cursing in English and Spanish. They saw a mountain of a man throwing an attractive woman in the back seat of a silver SUV, then getting in after her. Claudius and Angie continued to watch while the big man and woman tussled in the back seat as a dark-skinned slim man, that Claudius recognized as an associate of X's, hopped into the driver's seat and backed out of the driveway. Not wasting anymore time, Claudius stood up and climbed over the deck's wall, then helped Angie over. With cat like stealthiest they both moved across the wooden deck and into the house through the fractured portal. After Angie followed Claudius into the house, they came short just before 10 paces and stood rigidly at the sight. They saw the backs of two men with both hands on their sub machine guns aimed at who Claudius would guess was X but couldn't see him from the angle they were at. Claudius took two steps to the right bringing X into his line of vision. X could be seen standing picturesquely with a smug look on his face. Angie Wu squeezed the trigger of her pistol fast and first before Claudius was ready.

"PFFF! PFFF!" Angie's bullets hit the twin Fame in the neck and head. Fame tumbled forward but before he hit the floor Money dropped, spun, and sprang to his right moving between his brother Fame and their new assailants.

Money let off a barrage of automatic gun fire from the Mac10 as he launched his body through the air, "Boaf! Boaf! Boaf! Boaf! Boaf! Boaf!" The diagonal line of fire from the Mac10 mimicked Money's rise and fall while he was airborne. The bullet holes in the wall were like a line of connect the dots only to be interrupted by Angie Wu's body. Angie Wu had taken 4 slugs in her torso. Claudius caught the twin in the head twice when Money landed awkwardly from his lunge in the middle of a tuck and roll move.

Claudius continued to walk toward the already dead Money filling his body with bullets. PFFF! PFFF! PFFF! PFFF! PFFF!

X stood frozen in shock planted in the same exact same spot he was in before the bullets started flying. "Shit! Fuck! Gawd Damn!" he said as he patted his body up and down amazed that he wasn't shot, but as X registered the face that was behind the black and green paint, he realized what had just occurred. He was saved only to be killed minutes later by another.

Detective Way, as X knew him, was now cradling the head of the person who also was clad in all black clothing with a camouflage painted face. Claudius rocked Angie Wu back and forth weeping blatantly as he spoke to her in quiet whispers like he was lulling her to sleep.

After a short time of watching this scene, X mustard up enough courage to speak, "Detective?"

Claudius instantly cut him off, "This is all your fault! She's dead!"

X took a step forward pleading, "I'm sorry."

But Claudius stopped him in his tracks as he adjusted his aim at X's head, "Don't move again Muthafucker!"

Claudius' eyes dropped to look at Angie's face and he began to wail loudly, not attempting to hold his emotions back.

X, with his hands held high, attempted to talk to the distraught detective again.

"Detective...I understand...these same Punk Bitches just took the love of my life...my wife," X lowered his eyes from the hawk like gaze of Claudius before he continued, "and unborn baby from me!"

All the hate that Claudius had had for this man that stood before him just minutes' prior, had disintegrated. What was once one of the most significant hurdle in his life, killing X, now seemed irrelevant as he held on to his dead future wife.

Dropping the aim from his pistol off of X, Claudius fished in the side pockets of his fatigues. Pulling out a small ring of keys he tossed them to X.

"The Clara Lee...she's docked in the Seaford Marina...go get your girl and sail away from this life! Start over new!" Claudius Way bent his head down and kissed Angie Wu on the lips and stuck the muzzle of the silence

45 in his mouth and pulled the trigger!

A large amount of adrenaline coursing through X's body paralyzed him. His mind raced and sought desperately for answers.

"How and why am I still alive?" X asked himself. Hearing a grunt, X spun around fast, startled. To his surprise he found O.G. stepping on the wrist of the twin Fame whose hand was a mere inch from his diabolical Mac10. O.G. breathed heavily like he'd ran all the way to the house. He wore a wife beater, black and gold silk boxers, and a pair of butter Timbs. O.G. stared down the barrel of an AK 47 that he had aimed at the outstretched twin.

"HOLD! HOLD! HOLD!" X yelled as he hurried over to O.G.'s side.

"Don't kill 'em!" Both men looked down at the dying man.

X said, "If you want to live Fame...tell me what's going on. Tell me your boss' next move!"

Fame didn't say a word verbally as his blood glistened and flowed from his wounds onto the hardwood floor. But he did agree to X's ultimatum and pleaded for his life with his eyes as he looked up into X's eyes.

"O.G.!" X said while bending down and applying pressure to Fame's neck wound to stifle the bleeding, "call the paramedics from the landline."

"What?" O.G. asked.

"This Fucken Punk just tried to smoke you...right?" he asked as he looked around at the carnage for the first time.

"Who that?" O.G. asked, pointing to the Late Claudius Way and Angie Wu.

"Tell you later Bro," X said, "call the ambulance!"

O.G. went hesitantly into the kitchen where the phone was at but still looking all around trying to piece together what had happened. When O.G. was gone X looked back into the weak eyes of Fame and spoke direct and clear to him.

"The ambulance will be here soon. Tell me...what's the deal?"

X bent his neck down to hear the raspy and strained voice of Fame, who grind and gritted his teeth up against the pain he felt.

"They gonna...kill the Queen Bitch!" Fame said sucking in and blowing out air through his mouth, "so...they can get Ms. Rae."

X ripped open his button-down Sean John shirt, took it off and tied it snug around Fame's neck. O.G. came back into the room as X was finishing up the makeshift tourniquet.

"Dog!" O.G. said with the AK 47 resting against his shoulder as if it were a baseball bat, "they gonna be here in about five minutes. Let's kick rocks!"

X figured Fame had a fifty-fifty chance of living. X knew his head wound was a graze, but Fame's neck was different. It was a strong possibility that his carotid artery had been hit. X concluded that if Fame was strong enough to hold on for the paramedics, he would pull through.

"You owe me Famous!" X said as he stood and followed O.G. towards the French doors.

"Two to three minutes," O.G. yelled back at Fame before exiting the house, "they'll be here to fix you up!"

X and O.G. ran to O.G.'s black 1968 Camaro that was left idling from his haste to enter the house. They could hear sirens approaching as O.G. burned rubber down the country back roads.

"O.G.!" X said looking at his friend, "I know you know where Lana is...I understand why you kept it from me. I was acting like an Asshole. But we have to go get her, Kush and El Oso are gonna kill her Bro!"

O.G. looked back at X a long moment before he spoke. X blurted out, "She' my only relative, I'm not gonna hurt her!"

O.G. grinned, "Glad to have my boy back! I Know where she at!"

"Let's go!" X shouted.

Looking down at his appearance O.G. said, "Man...I gotta get some clothes X!"

KNOCK KNOCK

"What you want? Sista Vic asked as she turned her back and walked away from the guest that stood in her doorway.

"We just stopped by to see how you were doing," Isis replied as her and Kish followed Sista Vic into the small apartment. Sista Vic's apartment smelled as it always had, like a mixture of the sweet tantalizing aromas of cooked meat, herbs, spices, fruits, and vegetables.

"Huh!" Sista Vic grunted in response to Isis' statement. Sista Vic sat down in a chair at her small kitchen table and resumed what Isis figured she had been doing when they knocked on her door, which was snapping string beans.

"X about to get married," Sista Vic said feigning like snapping string beans took a lot of concentration. "I know you ain't around here lookin for him?" As soon as those words came out of Sista Vic's mouth she regretted saying them.

That was the first Isis had heard anything about X getting married, and Kish, as well as Sista Vic, could physically see that the news hit her like a hay maker. While Kish sat on Sista Vic's couch Isis stood frozen in her tracks, stunned and speechless. She wasn't so naive to think that she was the only woman in X's life. Isis reminded herself that the last time she had seen X Evita was with him. Isis clenched her teeth together tightly and wiped a tear from her eye.

Sista Vic tried to lighten the sting of the blow she had just delivered to Isis and apologize in her own way.

"I haven't heard from X in a couple days' child," Sista Vic said looking at Isis for the first time.

"I know y'all got some of that weed y'all can go ahead and smoke." Gaining her composure Isis pulled out a bag of weed and a blunt, then gave it to Kish to roll.

"I have somethin' for you too Sista Vic," Isis said as she handed Sista Vic a little plastic bag of Sista Vic's "so called" medicine.

Sista Vic grinned for the first time since they had arrived saying, "I always knew you loved me!"

"What's going on?" Icy Bezel asked an old white lady in her house coat and slippers. She was one of about 50 people standing behind the yellow police tape, trying to get a glimpse of a dead body and find out what had happened.

"Tragic! Just Tragic!" the old woman said shaking her head as she held her house coat cinched tightly. "I heard the sweet couple were soon to be married that lived here were both murdered..."

The old lady just like all the other spectators and Icy Bezel snapped their heads in the direction of the front door, as uniform men and women pushed three stretchers with completely covered bodies out and into a coroner's vehicle and paramedics.

The lady continued, "The bold young man did manage to kill the three intruders before he died, though."

"Do you know the couple that lived here?" Icy Bezel asked.

"No, not personally," the old lady said, "but I saw them just about every day. I live next door." Which wasn't actually next door but their two houses were separated by about 100 yards of woods.

"They looked happy and beautiful together." The old lady for the first time took her eyes off the crime scene to look up at the person asking the questions who obviously didn't live around here.

Icy Bezel noticed right away how the old lady stared at him, he could already imagine the gears turning in the little woman's head. The lady looked just like the type to be home still watching old re-runs of Murder She Wrote. Icy took that as his que and quietly slid off when the lady turned her attention back towards the different officers milling around.

Walking back to his car Icy Bezel couldn't help but notice the empty feeling in the pit of his stomach and heart. He couldn't identify the sorrow that he felt, it was foreign to him. Icy Bezel dug deep within himself and hardened his heart as he had no time to feel sorry for X being killed. Sliding into his car his cell phone rang. Looking at the screen he saw an unforgettable number that he hadn't seen in years.

"Hello?"

BACK AT LANA'S

"Come in! It's open!" Lana yelled when she heard a knock at the door. She didn't have to look up as she flipped card after card over playing solitaire. Lana knew who it would be that walked through her door, she was expecting him.

"Queen Bee," Kush distinctively smooth voice called out as he glided his way over and gave her a hug, then sat across from her.

"Lana it's good to see you..." Kush's smile vanished as he spoke, his features turning solemn, "but I'm afraid for your life, X will be here soon to kill you!"

In Lana's bedroom, O.G. had to restrain X back from bum rushing the scene prematurely once he heard Kush lie on him. O.G. held X behind the closed bedroom door quietly until he stopped struggling. Since Lana didn't trust X's word 100 percent in saying that Kush was coming to kill her, she made them wait in the other room until she was convinced and then she would give them a signal to come out.

"How will we know when you want us to come out?" O.G. asked as he and X scurried to Lana's bedroom when they saw Kush pulling up in the driveway.

"You'll know," Lana said calmly.

Kush continued, "X wants those codes from Ms. Rae, and he will stop at nothing...but I'll protect you, Lana..." Kush paused looking around. "Where is Ms. Rae? Both of you are in danger!" Lana finally stopped flipping cards to look at Kush.

"Come here," Lana said curling her index finger, indicating that she wanted him to come close. Confused, Kush slowly rose from his seat and crossed the short distance until he was inches from Lana. He stood over her as she still sat.

Looking up at him, Lana batted her eyes seductively and licked her lips slowly before she spoke, "I've been wanting to say this a long time."

As Lana was speaking, she reached out and circled her arms around Kush's waist with a head resting on his abdomen, "I wanted you ever since the first day I've laid eyes on you..." She giggled pleasantly while her hands rubbed, caressed, and massaged Kush's back. Kush had always wanted Lana but he knew X wouldn't approve.

His eyes twinkled with delight as he anticipated what was about to take place. *He said to himself, "Why not lay some wood, kill the Bitch and then get the codes from Ms. Rae. That's a plan!"* A smile broadened and he looked down at the exotic, deliciously looking Lana. A feeling of dread pushed its way past the euphoria Kush felt with another thought, of what Lana was trained by X to do. Seduce, rob, and kill!

"Where is Ms. Rae?" Kush asked raising his voice. Then he pushed Lana's hands off of him and went to retrieve his pistol that was stuck in the small of his back. His jaw went slack as his hand touches nothing but his bare skin.

"You treacherous Bitch!" Kush yelled looking into the barrel of his own pistol pointing up on him.

At hearing Kush yell, X and O.G. both shot out of Lana's room like they were racing. They punched and kicked Kush until they were out of breath and all he could do was moan as he laid bloodied, lumped, and bruised on the linoleum floor. Lana's eyes stayed on the trail of smeared blood that was made as O.G. on one side of him and X on the other, dragged Kush across the floor and up into a chair where they commenced to binding him with duct tape.

Isis and Kish were sitting at Sista Vic's kitchen table eating a huge breakfast early in the afternoon that Sista Vic had been up early in the morning preparing while the girls had slept off the partying, drinking, and smoking they had been doing over Sista Vic's for the past two days. Sista Vic was up thinking while she cooked, about what she could do to reconcile The Family that the boys she called her sons created. Isis and Kish's visit made Sista Vic realize how much she had missed the money, company coming and going, and most of all X, Kush, Sizzle, O.G. and Icy Bezel. Right then and there as she cooked, Sista Vic decided she would reach out to her sons and stop all this foolishness. First, she called X's phone but didn't get an answer, and got the same results for O.G. and Kush. She cursed out loud feeling discouraged about her failed attempt to fix her broken family as she dialed Icy Bezel's phone number.

Kish and Isis talked, as they ate their breakfast about the night before but was interrupted by a knock at the door that stopped them mid-sentence. The knock sounded like the "drum roll knock" that the girls heard X use. In the girl's stunned silence, Sista Vic shuffled to the door.

"Bezel!" Sista Vic screamed joyfully when she opened the door.

Ms. Rae arrived with Milli and the outfit she had gone to the store to get the almost naked O.G. just as X was finishing up securing Kush with duct tape to a chair. Lana sat quietly in her same spot at the kitchen table, but now smoking a blunt. Lana stroked Milli's head as it lay rested in her lap, she was thinking about how she couldn't wait to get the cast off her leg. She felt vulnerable for the first time since being raped by Nice. If it wasn't for her trust in O.G., who convinced her that X didn't want to harm her and that Kush was the true turn coat, Lana wouldn't have gone along with their plan to spring this trap for Kush.

"They were right!" she said to herself, *"Kush was coming to kill me,*

and he would have done it if X and O.G didn't come!"

Lana's thoughts were interrupted by X asking her to pass the blunt. Lana sucked her teeth at X and continued puffing.

"Oh, it's like that cuz?" X asked.

O.G. laughed as he was slipping on the pants that Ms. Rae had bought him. X didn't feel offended by Lana, he felt she had every right in the world to be angry with him. He did catch the quick smile Lana tried to hide, that told him that he was back in her good graces.

"Where's Isis and Kish?" O.G. asked neither Ms. Rae nor Lana answered him.

X could see by the two women's expressions that something had happened. He pressed, "What happened Lana?"

Lana exchanged looks with Ms. Rae and then said calmly, "They went looking for you."

After Lana took a couple more pulls off her blunt, she continued speaking. "The question is...what are we gon' do with him?" Lana asked nodding towards Kush.

Nobody in the room said anything as they all looked at the slumped Kush who sat bound and gagged. The large massive Milli heard it first. Her ears shot up then she stood then she sat up straight and growled. Seconds later, everyone could hear a car pulling into the yard.

"You expecting anyone?" X asked Lana.

Lana shook her head, "No!" Then grabbed the pistol off of the table that she had taken from Kush and cocked it.

Ms. Rae went into the living room so she could catch a glimpse of who it was that pulled into the yard from a window. She ran back into the dining room where Lana, X, and O.G. were, "Its Icy Bezel, Kish, Isis, and the old lady!"

THE FAMILY

Approximately four houses away from Lana's supposedly Safe House, sat a black Chevy Suburban with smoked windows and UHF antennas. Federal Agent Russel sat under the steering wheel with a pair of binoculars glued to his face while his partner Agent Rogers spoke into a cell phone to their superior.

"Yes, we're witnessing the founders of the Diamond State Mafia all at one place!" Agent Rodgers stopped speaking to listen to his boss bark out orders, he rolled his eyes and frowned his clean-shaven face up. That's all the agent dared do about not agreeing with what the boss delegated to him.

"Sir. Yes, Sir!" Agent Rodgers said, clearly disappointed as he ended the call.

"Told you," Russel said removing the binoculars from his eyes and looking over to his partner.

"Shut up!" Rodgers spat back, "he said Moore's still gathering evidence on these creeps!"

"What?" Russel asked shocked, then continued, "Agent Moore has been under deep cover for almost a year. I'm pretty sure we have enough to bury all of what's left of this so-called Family!"

"I agree," Agent Rodgers said, "I don't know why we haven't taken these killers, racketeers, and manufacturers off the streets. I just hope we'll shut 'um down before Agent Moore's identity is compromised!"

The Feds have been quietly building a case up against all of the members of The Family for at least two years. They coined the moniker

"Diamond State Mafia" for The Family. That name screamed out in bold red letters above a hierarchy in the shape of a pyramid with the names and pictures of each family member thumb tacked to a cork board in the team's headquarters. Agent Russel and Rodger's were part of a team of five. Including them, there was Hawkins and Clanton who were back at headquarters. Then there was Agent Moore, who had volunteered to infiltrate the first organized crime family in Delaware.

"Something big is going on in there and I'm..." Agent Rodgers jumped out of the SUV, leaving Russel shaking his head at his partners' disregard for following orders. Russel huffed and puffed but still grabbed their camera then got out of the Chevy quietly to folly his partner. O.G. opened the door for their unexpected guest. After he embraced Sista Vic, Kish, and Isis, O.G. turned making eye contact with Icy Bezel, letting his eyes drop and rest on the gun in Icy's hand. Icy Bezel nodded a "What's up!" to O.G. then tucked the pistol. O.G. locked the door then lead them to the dining room. Sista Vic gasped upon entering the dining room seeing Kush duck taped and beaten. She went straight to Kush and gently laid a hand on his swollen face, while everyone else watched in silence. Kush gingerly raised his head to look up at Sista Vic, pitifully.

"What's going on?" Sista Vic asked, "this is what it's come to? You let money, drugs, and power tear apart this Family!" Icy Bezel stepped forward.

"Sista Vic, X is doing the right thang. Kush was behind it ALL, the execution of Jesus to dividing us all up!" As Icy Bezel spoke, he circled the defenseless Kush.

"Me and Sizzle were right about him..." he paused, then looked at X.

"But we were wrong about thinking X was down with his treachery. I see now that you've found out how low this snake will crawl!" Icy Bezel back handed Kush, causing an instant gash to open up beneath his eye. All the women in the room cringed, accept Lana. She stopped stroking Milli's head then braced herself against the table as she stood. Milli rose up as well on all fours with a low growl.

"So, he's the cancer that has dismantled and almost destroyed what we all loved so much," Lana said with a voice devoid of emotion as she looked at everyone in the room, purposely letting her eyes rest on Kish and Isis a little longer, giving them both an evil eye.

"Just like the cancerous disease that we have to cut out...we have to do the same with him," Lana said pointing to Kush, "he needs to be eradicated...for the future of The Family!"

"X! Icy!" Sista Vic spoke, visibly shocked and hurt by Lana's request. "This is your Brother! I can't believe..." Sista Vic covered her mouth in disbelief at how easy it was for them to take a life, of someone that was so close. Seeing that X, nor Icy Bezel didn't object to Lana's call, Sista Vic searched all the faces in the room for leniency but found none. Sista Vic turned back to Lana, seeing that Kush's life was in her hands. "Please, don't do this Lanie...he's one of us!" Lana's cold exterior didn't falter, waver or grumble. Without giving Sista Vic a verbal response, her intent was made loud and clear.

"I remember the sweet innocent young lady Lanie that showed up at my door years ago," Sista Vic said sounding appalled and drained, "she's gone...you ARE the Queen Bitch I heard so much about...!"

Agent Rodgers and Russel peered through Lana's window into the living room that would be a dream for any lawman, but Agent Rodgers last orders were to not interrupt Agent Moore's infiltration of The Family. Agent Rodgers was afraid for the undercover agent's life, with him knowing from Moore's weekly check-ins of all the tension between the family members. The two agents watched on as Lavander Jones aka Icy Bezel strikes abound with duct tape to a chair that Hason Wallace aka Kush sat. Agent Rodgers scanned the room identifying all of the families' upper echelons and Agent Moore.

ABOUT THE AUTHOR

Kyleef Watts lives in lower Delaware. Before becoming an acclaimed writer, he led a life of crime. Now, with his checkered past behind him, he uses his experiences to paint vivid pictures for those that never witnessed firsthand the dynamics of the underbelly of society.